T0086324

SURVIVAL

CHRIS WOOTTON

authorHOUSE®

AuthorHouse™ UK
1663 Liberty Drive
Bloomington, IN 47403 USA
www.authorhouse.co.uk
Phone: UK TFN: 0800 0148641 (Toll Free inside the UK)
        UK Local: (02) 0369 56322 (+44 20 3695 6322 from outside the UK)

Published by AuthorHouse 10/26/2021

ISBN: 978-1-5462-9006-3 (sc)
ISBN: 978-1-5462-9025-4 (e)

Print information available on the last page.

CONTENTS

Chris Wootton was born in 1956 in Melbourne, Australia. For as long as he can remember, Chris has had a fascination for science fiction books and films and still enjoys re-reading the books of John Wyndham, Isaac Asimov and Arthur C Clarke. Chris is married and between having four daughters, three grandsons and four granddaughters, and his work in philanthropy, he has only just found time to begin writing science fiction, rather than just reading someone else's book! Nova follows Return of the Mistau as his latest science fiction.

KEY CHARACTERS

Otis Argyle – Atlai Base Operations
Dr Walter Basson – South Africa
Commander Buck Beckmann – USS Obama
Bill Bishop – President, Beekeepers Association of Australasia
Jim Bradley
Mary Bradley
Jackson Bradley
Bowie Bradley
Mr Brown – ASIO (Australian Security & Intelligence Agency)
Simon Bulwinkle – Chairman CIQ
Harvey Claire – Food Production Manager (Altai)
Sonia Claire – Head Chef (Altai)
Christine Claire – Utility Operations
Jonsey Day – Altai Base Operations
Dordain Dent
Sarah Dent
Kaylan Dent
Toyan Dent
Claire Dent
Corporal Jenny Fitzgibbon – Skylab XIII, Systems Specialist
Mr Gray – ASIO (Australian Security & Intelligence Agency)

Captain Gunn – Commanding Officer - Marines

Dr Peter Harris – Altai Base Doctor

Dr James Hawthorne - Veterinary Doctor

Sue Hendy - Dr Stolz's Receptionist

Sam James

Jenny James

David James

Graeme James Dr Ben Jones – USS Obama

Corporal Sue Jones – Skylab XIII, Communications Specialist Gus Lassiter – Mine Rescue, Chile

Commander Neil Lavarche – Skylab XIII

Dan Mars – Special Advisor to the President of the United States

Dr McKewan – British Museum

Patricia (Pat) Milner – Engineer in Chief (Altai)

Nancy Moore - Communications Centre (Altai)

General Oliver – US Military Special Projects

Dr Shaun Pike PhD (Spike) – USS Obama

Emperor Quaylan – Quanernia and on the New Dawn Dr Timothy Reid - Environmental Immunologist, Melbourne University

Frank Setaro – Altai Operations & Logistics Manager (Deputy)

Professor Sally Stewart – Astrophysicist, Palomar Observatory California

Dr Henry Stolz - Tinnitus Specialist, San Francisco Chris Vernon

Mandy Vernon

Jade Vernon

Nicole Vernon

Captain Wojinski – Altai Shuttle Pilot

chapter 1

2047

Pat Milner loved her job. She was good at it, and she knew it. She felt at home being at the cutting edge of engineering excellence, where-ever that may be. At this point in time the cutting edge was located at a depth of two kilometres below the surface, at the end of a six-kilometre-long shaft cut into a side of an ancient hill. This basaltic hill had remained mostly unchanged since it was created over 4.4 billion years ago.

Pat had lived most of her life in Florida, however she claimed that her family tree went all the way back to the original Welsh coal miners in the Rhondda Valley. Wales was famous for its coal mining industry which dated back to the period of Roman Empire occupation of the United Kingdom. Pat often cursed her Welsh heritage for her short stature, being just less than five feet tall. The only time she felt self-conscious about her height was when she was asked to speak at a conference, as she often needed a step stool so that she could see over the lectern!

Pat often wondered what the Welsh miners would

have thought of this mine if they could see it now. Unlike conditions in the 19th Century, mining no longer involved little squat men and often incredibly young children working with dynamite and pickaxes at the coal face.

When working late in her office, she would often swivel her chair to look at an old print hanging on the wall. It portrayed a group of miners emerging from a coal mine shaft, their faces and hands black with coal dust and soot from the oil lamps. Their clothes saturated with sweat from toiling in the hot and horribly cramped conditions. From stories that she had read, they constantly lived in fear of a collapse or an explosion from the gases which would build up in pockets of the shaft. They would take canaries in cages down into the mine as an early warning system for bad air. When the canary died, it was time to get out fast! In those days safety was not a priority for the mine owners as labour came cheap. Pat had memorised a well-known Welsh[1] mining song that had been hand-written on the back of the print. Now although almost unreadable as it had faded over time, it appropriately summed up a miner's life:

> *I am a little collier and working underground*
> *The rope will never break when I go up and down*
> *Its bread when I'm hungry*
> *And beer when I'm dry*
> *Its bed when I'm tired*
> *And heaven when I die*

The thought of needing to have canaries in this mine made Pat chuckle. Instead of pickaxes, Pat oversaw a huge and complex wave-bore drilling machine that could cut through solid rock at 40 metres per day. This monster was over 140 metres long with a cutting diameter of 25 metres and 300 plus teeth all rotating at 9.7 times per minute. The machine used a condensed sound wave to fracture solid rock and then high-speed cutters did the rest. The crushed rock, known as 'muck' in the trade, was then automatically deposited onto a conveyer belt which took it back up to the surface of the mine. This boring machine only required two operators. They sat comfortably inside the control room of the boring machine, in pressurized suits focussing on the monitors that constantly reported every working part. Jonsey and Otis were working this shift and Pat thought that they were the best team in the business. They had now worked together for several years and between them they could really make this big baby sing! This machine was a quantum leap from the first tunnel boring machine which cut the Fréjus Tunnel in the Alps between France and Italy back in 1846.

Pat had worked her way to the top the hard way. Despite the best efforts by women to balance the gender gap, engineering at the senior levels remained very male dominated. Being female, perceptions remained that to succeed meant that Pat had to be either twice as good as the next guy or sleep with the boss or both!

For all her life Pat hated, with a passion, to fail at anything. At school she always wanted to learn and as such was identified as the 'nerd' of the class.

To make matters worse, as well as her short stature, her eyesight was also poor so she had to wear a large pair of black rimmed glasses due to the thick size of her lenses.

Pat hated every minute of wearing them at school as she was constantly teased and bullied by others. Officially, bullying had been eradicated at all schools, but even now it was still rife in many schools. Looking back on it now, Pat thought it was strange how life can be turned around, as her choice of large black rimmed glasses was now her most distinguishing trademark in business. Everyone knew of her by these glasses. Some aspiring female engineers had even copied her and wore the exact same pair of glasses! She also hated her full name, Patricia, and often glared at people when they called her by her full name. 'It's Pat, just Pat!' she would have to say repeatedly.

And watch out if anyone would dare call her Patty!

All her life Pat had found it hard to make good friends and as such she never felt like she belonged, until she entered university and studied engineering. Engineering was her first real love. Pat found mathematics easy and jobs were opening in space-related engineering. Space, the final frontier was finally emerging as the new reality, and she found herself right in the middle of it. She just could not believe her luck to be living during this time in Earth's history!

Pat excelled at university and was placed in the top three students of her class at the University of California and virtually had the chance to go to any job she wanted once she graduated. However, Pat was not interested in just any job, she had set her sights on Stanford University where she wanted to do a PhD. And Pat always got what she wanted!

It was just the week prior to Pat moving to Stanford that her parents were tragically killed in an horrific motor vehicle accident. Pat's brother had died young, and her parents were her 'rock'. As expected by everyone, she very efficiently managed all the funeral arrangements and did not shed a tear during the service, even when delivering a very moving eulogy. However, it was about two days later when grief finally hit her badly. Pat found herself crying for hours and she hardly left her small apartment for weeks at a time. Her malaise lasted for nearly twelve months over which time she did absolutely nothing, apart from function on the most basic of levels. She deferred her place at Stanford, which really meant that she would never get there. She also completely ignored all the lucrative job offers from recruiters who still chased her. She would not return their calls and after a while they gave up.

She had already given up on herself long ago!

It had been a day just like any other since the funeral when Pat woke up in a daze and crawled out of bed after another night of heavy binge drinking. She looked at the clock and noticed without much surprise that it was 3pm. She heard her phone ring and she stumbled into the lounge room, picked up her phone and looked to see who had called and left her a message. She realised that the television must have been left on all night, again!

The phone call was from her only real friend, Dan Mars. While they were in totally different faculties at University, Dan studied economics and commerce and was Dux of his graduating class. They often hung out at the library and held their own interactive and challenging tutorial sessions. Dan's phone message was brief and merely told her to turn on the television and wait for a news item about Chile. She tossed her phone back on the couch and was about to return to her bedroom when she decided why not, the television was still on anyway.

After flicking though a few channels, she finally came to one which began as a simple story about an Australian engineer by the name of Gus Lassiter who had just flown to Copianpó Chile. Pat assumed that this must be what Dan had told her about. The reporter went on to say that Gus was going to help save a group of miners who were trapped deep underground in one of the world's oldest gold mines. The reporter then went on to explain, 'They will be using a new technique called wave-rock mining. This is an extremely fast way to cut through solid rock using sound waves to break down basic rock structures. The rescue team intend to cut a whole new shaft to get these men out alive. What would have been impossible only a couple of years ago is now possible.' And then the news went on to report on a multiple murder in a restaurant in downtown Paris.

From that moment on, Pat knew what she wanted to do. It was like a lightbulb going off in her head! She checked to see what she had left in her bank account and booked a one-way shuttle ticket to Chile. She knew that she just had to go and work for this man named Gus.

The shuttle fight was comfortable and after a rough four-hour drive in a hired 6WD Landcruiser she finally arrived at the entry gate to the Copianpó mine site. It looked like a scene from the movie 'Apocalypse Now' with television helicopters, vans and cameras everywhere! It took a long time for her to convince security at the gate that she was neither a distraught relative nor another over-energetic journalist. Finally, after a lot of heated discussion in a mixture of broken English and Spanish they let her in; nothing was going to stop Pat anyway!

After a long wait at the Rescue Site HQ, she was finally introduced to the boss, Gus Lassiter. While Gus was totally bemused that anyone should fly thousands of kilometres to come and help without letting anyone know in advance, he really did need all the help that he could get!

It did not take long for Pat to demonstrate her usefulness as she was able to make several modifications to the wave-boring machine which increased its boring efficiency by more than 20 per cent. Within two weeks of constant drilling, they were able to rescue all the trapped miners alive and well. Gus was an instant international celebrity and by default Pat enjoyed the ride. In those two weeks Pat learnt more about mining than she had ever learnt at university. That was not all she learnt, as Gus was great in bed and was Pat's first lover. But Pat really wanted more than just Gus' body; she wanted everything that was in his head!

After a torrid love affair lasting just over 12 months and working in mining disaster sites in three different continents, Pat found that she now knew enough to go her own way. There was just nothing left from Gus for her to learn! They both parted ways on good terms with Gus realising that his world was just too small to contain someone like Pat.

Using what she had learned about wave-rock technology and boring machines, Pat added her own further improvements and went looking for new and more challenging adventures. Whilst working on a Chevron deep drilling oil project in Antarctica, she met Simon Bulwinkle, Chairman of an international conglomerate mining company CIQ, which was worth an estimated $700b US dollars. Simon was already well past the age of retirement and was more than 50 years older than Pat. But for Pat, Simon was loaded with great business acumen, money and political connections. Whilst Simon was a true entrepreneur, he did not stand a chance against Pat once she decided what she wanted. She was like a whirlwind and just swept him off his feet, both physically and mentally. As you would guess, Simon's family and friends immediately hated Pat as they could see what Pat was doing and they did not like it at all. The more they had tried to tell Simon, the more he argued against them. This only improved Pat's chances of getting what she wanted. Finally, Pat had her way and despite the protestations of the family they were married in the Cayman Islands and honeymooned on Skylab XI. The last few Skylab's, once decommissioned, had been totally refurbished as luxury space hotels. Skylab XI had been operating as a hotel for several years with 100 hotel suites. They offered guests not only the best that Earth had to offer, but the Earth as well! At least that is what the marketing material told prospective guests at $5M per night, per person, plus the cost of the Virgin Galactic Shuttle flight!

Pat was more than enough to wear down any man, and Simon proved no different. He died suddenly from a massive heart attack only two months after their wedding! Pat did not waste any time mourning for Simon as once his affairs had been settled by the courts, she immediately took over as Chairman of CIQ and put his amassed fortune to good work. Pat retained the title of *Chairman*, rather than the more common *Chair*, as she felt it recognised her as being better than any man, and the title of Chairman just reinforced this to everyone else. As Chairman, Pat reorganised the company and invested billions into further developing wave-rock technology. CIQ gained the reputation of being at the leading edge of mining in the most difficult terrains.

So, when a project called Altai was proposed, Pat did everything she could to make sure CIQ won the tender to construct it!

Pat now oversaw the most ambitious engineering project ever constructed by mankind and all delivered and operated by the private sector.

Pat suddenly was jolted back into reality, as in the background the revolutions of the drill-head had begun to slow down indicating that it was time to call it quits after another long shift. The next crew would already be on their way down to take over shortly. She made her way out from the control compartment and was already seated securely on the staff train, which ran parallel to the gravel conveyor belt, when Jonsey and Otis joined her as they began the slow six-kilometre ride back up to the surface. Jonsey and Otis had lost count of the number of times they had traversed this ride back and forth. Being so busy, Pat was rarely able to visit the mine site, but felt that it was very important to see how the machine and her staff were performing. She never liked to lose touch with the pointy end of any project.

Pat's heart began to race as she could see daylight at the end of the shaft as they drew closer. For Pat, the view at the end of this ride was always worth it. As they exited the shaft there to greet them was the Earth, in all its glowing blue glory. It never ceased to amaze her and give her goosebumps!

Project Altai, Mankind's first colony on the Moon was the most incredible feat since the first landing on the moon back in 1969, nearly 80 years ago. And Pat's work had made it all possible.

At this point in time, Pat could never have imagined just how important to the survival of humanity that Project Altai would ultimately prove!

chapter 2

BENDIGO (AUSTRALIA)

It was another stinking hot day in Bendigo, a regional satellite city located north-west of Melbourne, Australia. The further geographic expansion of Melbourne had been capped by the early 2030's and all future population growth was moved to regional centres like Bendigo, which now had a population of over 3 million. Australia, often called the 'lucky country' had experienced unprecedented population growth because of massive refugee intakes arising from the extended series of regional conflicts and civil wars during 2030 to 2040. Australia was seen by the world, and especially by the United Nations, as a haven with massive potential to house and feed a much larger population. From 2030 to 2040, the population had increased from 30 million to nearly 100 million which had caused all sorts of political, social and environmental issues.

Kaylan Dent was walking home from school, like any other day, after being dropped off by the school bus. He enjoyed school but found it hard to make friends as his family had moved house so often. Kaylan was in his last year at Bendigo Secondary College even though it was his sixth school in nine years. Despite changing schools so often, Kaylan was still able to keep up with his leaning due to his excellent academic ability. He was also fortunate that he had been able to attend schools that still had real teachers, rather than on-line robotic teachers as most city-based students had to endure. His favourite subjects were mathematics and computer analytics and it did not take him long to realise that he knew more about computer code than any of his teachers and robotic tutors. He loved the flow and rhythm of computer codes and to him writing code was like playing music.

Kaylan lived with his mother, Sarah, on a small property just over fifty kilometres to the north of Bendigo. It took the school bus over one hour for a one-way trip where it dropped him off at a gravel lane. Kaylan then had to walk nearly a kilometre along this lane up to his home. Kaylan loved living in the country rather than in the very over-crowded cities. On their property they had a few Alpacas, pigs, cows, chickens and a huge walled vegetable garden so they were mostly self-sufficient. Like most properties they generated their own solar electricity and biofuels. Kaylan's father had left unexpectedly when he was only a baby. And when Kaylan raised the subject of his father, his mother would refuse to talk about him. As such, Kaylan had given up asking and he assumed that he must be dead.

One day as Kaylan was walking home his thoughts focussed on a problem, one that had only started recently and seemed to be getting worse. What had started out as being an occasional ringing noise in his head when he was in a shopping centre or just walking down a busy street, was now getting unbearably loud. However, this day whilst on a school excursion to the Bendigo International Science Museum, the ringing noises had started again. At first because they were so loud, he thought that everyone must be able to hear them. On looking around he quickly realised that no one else could hear anything strange. The ringing noises, just like before, were only in his head. Only this time they were so loud that he could not even hear the tour guide or his teacher above the noise. So, as he tried to focus on the ringing noise, he found that it increased and decreased in intensity and sounded more like a static-electrical noise, like when you turn a dial to change the frequency on a CB-radio.

Previously when he had told his mother about these noises in his head, she told him to try and ignore them and hope that they would go away. But they had not, and he found that they were getting more frequent and much louder.

So, Kaylan had decided when he got home that he would raise it again with his mother and perhaps he would need to see a doctor. It was only then that Kaylan realised that whilst the kids at school always talked about seeing a doctor, he could not actually remember ever going to one. He knew he must have been to one, but it must have been a while ago when he was too young to remember. With that thought in mind, he walked through the home gate and as usual his mother was sitting on the steps of the veranda waiting for him. Kaylan always thought that his mother must sit for hours on the step, as no matter when he arrived home from school, even when he was late, his mother would always be there waiting for him, 'Hi darling, how was school today?'

Kaylan was about to give his usual response, 'Ok', when he decided to try again about the noises, 'Mum I think I had better go and see a doctor.'

'Why, what's wrong?'

'The noises were really bad today.'

'That's no good. Can you hear them now?'

'Nope, actually I don't think that I have ever heard them at home.'

'Well, that is strange then. Perhaps you should keep a diary of when you hear the noises and then we would have something to take to the doctors.'

With a plan resolved, Kaylan walked inside to watch some television before tea.

Kaylan's mother remained on the steps and her expression changed to reflect her concern. Quietly she said to herself, 'It's starting, it really is starting, but he is still so young. I wonder why now?'

chapter 3

NEWCASTLE (AUSTRALIA)

Dr James Hawthorne was a highly experienced veterinary surgeon based in Newcastle, which is located on the central coast of New South Wales, Australia. His speciality was thoroughbred horses and his clientele lived in the high-quality horse country in the Hunter Valley Region. Not only did he enjoy his work, but he was extremely well paid for it.

Today he was visiting an old friend, Bill Bishop, whom he had known since school days. 'At least,' he muttered to himself, 'I don't have to think about work.' So often he would visit his friends, only to be asked to look at their pet dog or cat and expected to provide free advice. Nothing annoyed him more. Bill was a good friend who worked with bees and was also the President of the Australian Bee-Keepers Association. Bees were something that as a vet there was no need to 'treat', until today that is!

After the usual friendly pleasantries and talking about Aussie Rules Football and the weather over a few cold beers, Bill turned to James with a serious look on his face and said, 'Look mate, I don't know what you know about bees, but I have a problem.'

'What sort of problem can you have with bees for Christ-sake Bill?'

'Well,' Bill said scratching his head, 'It seems that they are all dying and bloody quickly too! In the past we have had all sorts of situations where bees die, but these have usually occurred in specific locations, or within a specific bee species. However, I am hearing reports from my members across Australia that their bees are dying. In fact, whole hives are dying within days which is totally unheard of. I think that this may be a new infection or biological disaster. On behalf of our members, I have sent samples of dead bees to government labs for analysis. So far, all the results have come back as inconclusive.'

Scratching his head, Bill continued, 'But I feel that we are getting the run around and I am now convinced that the authorities must know something but are keeping it quiet. So, mate, while I know you do not deal with bees, I'm hoping that you may know someone who could look at these dead bees and see if they can work out what may be happening.'

James could see that Bill was genuinely concerned and as he handed him another beer he continued, 'From your experience mate, do you have any ideas?'

'Really, I think it may have something to do with the tiny mites that live on the legs of bees. I have been searching the net, chat rooms, obscure blogs and tweets and when you try and put it all together, it is not just only happening here in Australia. It seems to be happening in the United States and in other countries. Earlier this year in California over 2,500 square kilometres of small almond nut trees were meant to be pollinated by millions of bees - that just did not arrive. That is half a billion kilograms of nuts, worth US$30 billion! Originally it was recorded as the worst loss of honeybees in the history of the industry. What was weird about this is that in the past three months there has been absolutely nothing in the media about it! Then again in the states, there were a few stories about the loss of more than 35 per cent of the population of the Western honeybee, better known as the *Apis mellifera* which had all died mysteriously. That is billions of individual bees which simply flew from their hives and died. The story in the media described a fancy new name for the problem, they called it a *Colony Collapse Disorder* and developed a list of official possible symptoms. A whole lot of symptoms were described in the protocols. They blamed it on a collapse of the bees' immune system caused by stress due to drought, viruses, introduced parasites, or new pesticides. But I think the government may be just using this 'disorder' to play the whole thing down and hide the truth from us.'

'So, what is the real cause and where do you think these mites may fit in?'

'With the so-called *Colony Collapse Disorder*, it has been claimed that adult worker bees simply flew away and died, resulting in the collapse of the hive. Talking to some of our members they are saying that all the bees are dying in the hive. Adding to this mystery, the usual bee predators, such as the wax moth, which just love feeding on bees, are even refraining from moving in to pilfer honey and other hive contents from the abandoned hives. Indicating perhaps that something is not right in the hive.'

'How bad do you think it is?'

'We've never seen such a die-off of this magnitude with this weird symptomology. In addition, I do not think we have ever seen whole hives die so quickly. It now threatens the very survival of the pollination industry. I am afraid that we must find the cause and quickly, otherwise we will have no more bees. And I will not have an association, nor a job for that matter!'

'So, what do you have there for me?' Said James pointing under Bill's chair.

'I have a sample of some of the dead bees. I have looked at these more closely under the microscope and the bees are covered in exceedingly small mites. At first, to me they looked like the common Asian mite, also known as the *Varroa* destructors.'

'Great name by the way!' Chipped in James with a grin.

'However,' continued Bill without pausing, 'when you look more closely, they are nothing that I have ever seen before. In fact, they are even more ugly than the Asian mites. They appear circular in shape, almost crab-like and about a tenth of the size of a bee's eyeball. I am calling the mites *Vegemites* and I think that they are a new and extremely deadly species of mite.'

'Okay okay, you've convinced me. If you give me another beer, I will take your bag of dead bees. I know of a good entomologist at Melbourne University who should be able to identify this mite via DNA testing and see just what you have in here!'

After a couple of hours of chatting and downing a few more beers, Dr Hawthorne finally made his way home with the bee sample bag tucked under his arm. Later that same week he posted off the sterile package containing the mites to a Dr Timothy Reid, a bug specialist at Melbourne University. Dr Reid had gone through university with Dr Hawthorne and they had kept in contact over the years.

chapter 4

MELBOURNE (AUSTRALIA)

Two week later, Dr Reid finally called James by Vidlink.

'Hi James, hope you are well. So sorry to take so long to get back to you, but you know how short-staffed we poor university staff are these days.'

'Whinge whinge whinge, you university people are all the same,' laughed James.

'Thanks for the package you sent me. I was so surprised when I opened it to find dead bees. I was not aware that the vet business was getting so desperate for work!

'I suppose I deserved that, Tim!

'Anyhow we have now completed the tests and I am pleased to confirm that the mites found on the dead bees are just a more virulent mutation of the common Asian mites we already have across Australia. However, it appears that this species of mites can be very nasty indeed, as they suck the vital juices out of both developing and adult bees and if left unchecked could kill a whole hive. Fortunately, it would take months or even years to affect a whole hive so with early detection your mate Bill's members should have time to kill these mites and save the hive. Sorry mate, but I must go now, so if there is anything else you need just let me know. I will send you the full official report shortly, so bye for now, and give my regards to Mary and the kids.'

The Vidlink screen suddenly went blank as the connection ended.

On the other end of the link, Dr Hawthorne still wanted to ask more questions, but just sat shocked and motionless staring at a blank screen. Normally, even when he was flat out working, Tim was far more talkative when they had the chance. His last words were even weirder, as Tim knew that he had never been married and had no kids, to his knowledge. Also, Bill had made it clear that whole hives were dying in days, not months or years!

James immediately tried to call Tim back, but there was no answer. Well, he thought, there was nothing he could do right now and he decided to wait to see the full report before contacting Bill with the strange results.

Standing behind Dr Reid and outside the viewing range of the Vidlink were two men dressed in dark suits. 'Thank you, Dr Reid, for being so helpful. We need to take those samples and your report and ask that you now delete all files related to this work. You have been very understanding and we now expect you to forget that this ever happened, and that we were never here!'

Dr Reid was not really listening, as it was more like a bad movie. He was thinking about all the news reports and blogs by his colleagues in the field since he had received and tested the samples. He still could not believe his results, yet his colleagues were also coming to the same conclusions. However, one by one their blogs and emails were systematically removed, along with the stories of complete bee colonies dying, as if they had never happened. He felt dreadful lying to his old friend James, but he had no choice. He hoped that he had given enough hints to his friend that not all was correct, without giving it away to the two ASIO agents.

After testing and re-testing, what he had found defied belief. At first, he thought that the lab had made an error, so he had passed the specimens onto another lab for independent verification. The tests were now conclusive, the mites from NSW were not made of the same genetic material found anywhere on Earth. They were completely of alien origin with DNA sequences never seen before. As to how these mites had come to Earth and the mechanism by which they killed bees so quickly, he and his colleagues had no idea.

Over the past couple of days, he had been conversing with his colleague Dr McKewan at the British Museum in London to verify his findings. He had also made the connection between this new species of mite and the death of bees. They both used the same term *Vegemite*, as named by James' friend Bill as their code for this new alien mite that was decimating bee colonies around the world.

In addition, Dr McKewan and other colleagues had started to see tests which indicated that this mite was mutating and moving to other species, such as mice, rates, chickens and birds, with potentially new deadly outcomes.

As one of the agents picked up the bee sample bag, Dr Reid was momentarily distracted by a beep from his computer and he could see that it was new message from Dr McKewan.

Dr Reid was puzzled at first, for as he starred at his screen the monitor was splattered in red, and as it dripped down the screen his eyes focussed on one particularly large drip as it quickly flowed down the screen. His last conscious thought was about how he might clean up the mess before his head fell lifelessly onto the keyboard.

The two agents left quietly, gently closing the office door behind them.

chapter 5

LONDON (ENGLAND)

Dr McKewan had been trying for days to contact Dr Reid as he now had no doubt that *Vegemites* were a new species of mites and that they were systematically decimating the world's bee population. From further discussions with his colleagues, it was also clear that *Vegemites* were mutating rapidly and targeting a wide range of other species and that authorities were deliberately covering up these events.

He tried one more time to call Tim but as he was now running late for work, he decided he would try again from his office, where he could use a more secure line.

Unfortunately, as it turned out he would never make that call.

As usual, he travelled to work on the tube and along with the mass of commuters climbed the steps from Tottenham Station and made the short walk to the British Museum. He did not notice a black van that had been parked on the curb pull out into the peak hour traffic in Charing Cross Road. Just as he stepped out onto the road the van sped up and swerved and struck him heavily from behind. Lying injured on the road he immediately thought how lucky he was, whilst in some pain, he also knew he was alive.

He then heard someone near him scream and at the time thought it was strange and then he knew why. From the corner of his peripheral vision, he saw the dark shape of the black van reversing back over him.

Had Dr McKewan still been alive, he would have heard the scream continuing as the mysterious black van sped off leaving his body in the middle of the carriageway. All traffic stopped as people milled around the scene. The BBC news that night carried a short story about a callous hit-and-run accident which had occurred just outside the British Museum during the morning peak hour which caused the death of the eminent scientist Dr McKewan, aged 47, leaving a wife and two children. Police were calling for any eyewitnesses to the accident to come forward.

chapter 6

CIQ HEADQUARTERS SAN DIEGO (UNITED STATES)

The main purpose of Project Altai involved the mining of Helium-3 for its use in nuclear fission. All the dire forecasts of the impact of climate change on the planet were now a reality and had occurred well in advance of even the worst predictions. Originally climate predictions expected global temperatures to rise by 2 degrees Celsius, however despite all efforts, it had increased by 6 degrees and was still rising. The polar ice pack at the North Pole was now only a thin layer of ice even in the depths of winter and the South Pole ice cover had reduced by over 80 per cent and would be gone in another 5 years. As a result, sea-levels had risen and inundated many Pacific islands and most low-lying coastal areas. Where possible, engineering lessons learnt from the Netherlands were employed and huge sea walls had been constructed to hold back rising sea levels in most major coastal cities. All fossil fuels were banned from use and Net Zero (Energy, Emissions & Water) was now globally mandatory. Alternative energy sources, whilst promising everything for a green future, had failed to deliver the energy needs of a growing and hungry planet. Even by the early 2030's nuclear power became the only viable solution. New ways to develop cleaner nuclear energy were showing some progress as governments around the world tried to meet energy demand for their own political survival. This is where Pat saw the opportunity of a lifetime.

During the days of the Apollo space program, in addition to returning with the all-important rock samples, they had also detected vast quantities of Helium-3 on the Moon[3]. The key benefit of Helium-3 was that when it is used in the nuclear fusion process, it did not produce radioactive waste as all the neutrons were consumed during the process. As an added benefit, Helium-3 also generated vastly more energy than traditional fission reactors. The only problem with Helium-3 was that it was extremely rare on Earth. At the beginning of Pat's work in this area, the cost to refine and develop Helium-3 was totally prohibitive.

However, the Moon contained an almost unlimited quantity of Helium-3!

More by chance, it was fortunate for Pat and her company CIQ, that neither the Government of the United States nor the United Nation's had ever ratified the 1984 original Moon Treaty. This treaty had sought to clarify space mining rights, by stating: "*The Moon and its natural resources are the common heritage of mankind,*" and that use of the moon, "*shall be carried out for the benefit and in the interests of all countries.*" Had this treaty been ratified, there would have been no way that CIQ could ever do what Pat proposed. Luckily for Pat (although she never believed in luck) she knew people in high places. Initially she made sure that this treaty stayed dead so that there would be no impediment for what CIQ and the Government of the United States really wanted to do.

She worked hard and positioned CIQ as the only engineering company with the equipment and know-how to conduct mining operations on the moon. Pat knew that the mining of Helium-3 was going to be a relatively simple process as it mainly consisted of a combination of conventional strip mining and underground boring techniques to mine the rich seams of Helium-3.

Underground mining also had a double whammy advantage on the Moon. Firstly, once the mining was completed, the mined area could then be easily adapted and used for future housing or storage. Initially being a simple open-cut mine, housing and other facilities could be built and then reburied with the mine waste and would be safe from solar radiation, asteroids and extreme temperatures. On the Moon's surface, temperatures could vary from 134 degrees down to minus 153 degrees.

Once the Helium-3 rich rock was extracted and broken down it was then heated, releasing the Helium-3. The Helium-3 could then be pumped into large reusable polythene bags ready for transfer down to Earth.

Part of the pre-positioning by CIQ involved the purchase of the Texas-based Shackleton Energy Company which had already begun research into mining the Moon within the next few years. With Pat's help they developed revised plans for mining and refining operations that involved melting the ice that had been discovered in craters on the dark side of the moon and converting the water into gaseous hydrogen and oxygen. The gases were then condensed into liquid hydrogen, liquid oxygen and hydrogen peroxide, all potential rocket fuels. Rocket fuel was essential to support and transport the team of people that would be required to operate a mine on the Moon. The mining and living components in fact were the easiest elements for Pat's team to solve. The major hurdle that they faced was how to transport the Helium-3 back to Earth in the most cost-effective way.

Pat's team of scientists and NASA solved one of the problems. When the Moon orbited between the Sun and Earth, a solar wind was created between the Moon and the Earth. The plan involved the creation of a huge sail, which could ride on the solar wind. The sail would be connected to a train of polythene bags, and once moving would simply glide to Earth. Some simple thrusters were added to keep the train on the right trajectory and then to slow it down once it entered a safe Earth orbit. Once tested, they found that they could transport a full payload of Helium-3 in just under 48 hours at minimal cost. An accountant's and shareholder's dream project!

However, the most complex and costly element was how to transfer the Helium-3 down to the Earth's surface. Pat's scientists explored low-cost shuttles that could collect the polybags and glide them down to the surface. However, the cost of flying the shuttles back up into orbit to collect the bags was still highly prohibitive and at one stage seemed to be a potential block to the whole project. It was a call from her old university colleague Dan Mars, who conveniently was now Special Advisor to the US President. Dan suggested that it would be a good idea to meet with a General Oliver.

So, she did! To Pat, General Oliver was the personification of the traditional military general. He was wearing the full regalia with coloured medals virtually covering half of his enormous chest. Every piece of metal and buttons on his impressive military tunic were so highly polished that Pat could see her own reflection!

After the usual pleasantries, and being a General he took the lead, 'Now before we begin, I would appreciate if we both agreed that this conversation never took place,' and he only continued after Pat nodded in approval, 'as what I am about to tell you is known by only a select few, apart from the President and of course my team who have been working on this secret project for many years. It is the biggest military research project since the Manhattan and Moon Landing Projects. We are building what has been called an Earth Elevator[4]. It is almost funny to think that such a major project is really based on a book, a concept that was first brought to life and made popular by that science fiction author Arthur C Clark in a novel called *The Fountains of Paradise*. Have you read it?'

Without waiting for Pat's response, the General went on to explain, 'Well the idea of a Space Elevator or Earth Elevator has been around since 1960 when a Russian, Yuri Artsutanov, wrote a Sunday supplement to Pravda on how to build such a structure making use of a geosynchronous orbit. His article, however, was not known in the West, and our people missed it, damn fools! We, I mean the military only became interested in 1966 when a John Isaacs, a leader of a group of American Oceanographers at Scripps Institute, also published an article in Science magazine about using thin wires hanging from a geostationary satellite that the concept became popular. However, the idea remained on paper as we did not have materials of the appropriate strength and flexibility to build this damn thing.' At first Pat did not know where this rambling conversation was going. She had read about the concept but in her opinion, it was still pure fantasy and impossible to engineer.

'Excuse me General, but did you say "did," what's changed?'

Then the General went on to explain, 'Look Pat, I see the scepticism on your face, but the space race is on again. China has just announced that they are about to expand their Chinese Lunar Exploration Program (CLEP). This program is going to consist of mining and the development of cities on the Moon. We must beat them! We need you to beat them! We know what you are trying to do and some of the immense problems you are facing. But Pat, let me tell you now, that Uncle Sam is here, and we will pay for your missing link, the Earth Elevator.'

Pat did not know what to say, in fact she could not even remember saying goodbye to the General or leaving his offices.

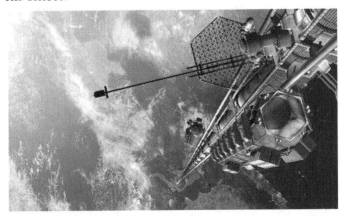

chapter 7

NAURU (PACIFIC OCEAN)

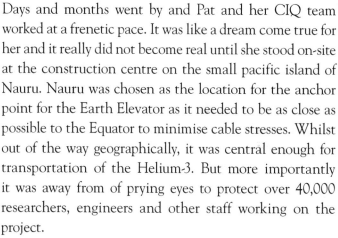

Days and months went by and Pat and her CIQ team worked at a frenetic pace. It was like a dream come true for her and it really did not become real until she stood on-site at the construction centre on the small pacific island of Nauru. Nauru was chosen as the location for the anchor point for the Earth Elevator as it needed to be as close as possible to the Equator to minimise cable stresses. Whilst out of the way geographically, it was central enough for transportation of the Helium-3. But more importantly it was away from of prying eyes to protect over 40,000 researchers, engineers and other staff working on the project.

Money was no longer an issue, only time was their enemy. The General's only interest and motivation was to beat the Chinese to the moon, so the space race was on again in earnest! As Pat knew, the greatest impediment to mining on the Moon was not the extremities of space but getting the mined materials back to the surface of the Earth in the most cost-effective way. The concept of the

Earth Elevator made this all possible, but she still thought that it was an engineering impossibility.

Again, the General had another surprise up his sleeve for Pat, and she was not one to be surprised very often. Her team was given access to the specifications of a top-secret material which had been developed by the military. To transport the Helium-3 to the surface of the Earth required the Earth-Elevator to be constructed as a long flexible snorkel which was attached to a hub-facility located in a geostationary orbit around 250 kilometres above the Earth. The specifications of this new secret material now made construction of the snorkel possible. Pat was surprised just how strong this new material was, and it was incredibly strong, and it had to be! But it also needed to be flexible enough to withstand the differing environmental conditions of temperature and other stresses. The hub required additional thrusters to maintain its close orbit to the Earth and to reduce any strain on the snorkel itself. Any error or malfunction, and the whole hub and snorkel would fall back to Earth or break, or the hub could just fly off into space.

In the end, the whole construction process went smoothly, despite the complexities. The hub was launched into space from Nauru with guide cables tethered to the ground and then set in position in orbit. Then the snorkel itself was constructed from the ground-up using a robotic unit which used the guide cables to creep forever upwards creating the snorkel membrane as it climbed like a 3-D printer. The Space Sails were constructed at Skylab XIII and tested so that shuttles from the Earth to the Moon and back could be conducted regularly, transferring people and materials needed to develop Altai and the first mine.

chapter 8

ALTAI (MOON)

Altai base was an engineering marvel. So as not to waste anything, the site for Altai itself was located within a rich seam of Helium-3. The basic design of Altai consisted of one wheel at the top and two smaller wheels connected offset underneath. Construction utilised one of the early open cut mines, which was wide and deep enough to contain the three wheels, making a total depth of nearly 60 metres, the equivalent of an eight-story building. The different wheels were identified as Penthouse, Lower A and Lower B. The Penthouse level housed the communications centre, cafeteria, library & recreation spaces, laboratories and core offices. Lower-Level A housed all accommodation and storage and Lower-Level B contained the nuclear reactor, high security section, an emergency bunker, water storage tanks and plant equipment for producing oxygen, recycled water and waste. The whole base was then buried under a further 20 metres of rock for added protection. This depth was considered by the experts as safe to withstand most of the dangers posed by living on the Moon, except perhaps for a direct meteor strike. On the surface there was a small portal which was connected via an airlock to the central core below along with landing pads, shuttle bunkers, solar panels, biofuel plant and an enormous self-enclosed greenhouse the size of three football fields.

Much to Pat's and even General Oliver's surprise, combined with a lot of sleepless nights, Altai was fully operational two years ahead of schedule by late 2045. Helium-3 was now in full production on the moon and shipments were regularly arriving on Earth every four days to keep a power-hungry planet alive!

Pat was that kind of person that could never stop, even whilst working on such a huge project. She also funded a range of new enhancements including Automatic Space Robots (ASR), which were primarily based at the Hub to manipulate the large polythene bags and transfer them into the top of the Earth Elevator snorkel. Through a combination of suction and gravity, the bags of Helium-3 merely fell to the collection point at Nauru, to be transported by sea to nuclear plants around the globe. Whilst the Earth Elevator was only able to function as a one-way trip, namely down. Pat assigned a small team of scientists to work on a way to allow vertical movement up the shaft. However, despite spending billions of dollars a solution still eluded them.

Pat had been the commander of Altai for nearly seven years and now was responsible for the 200 people and their families who called Altai home. Altai could accommodate up to around 300 people. Altai was totally self-sufficient for food and water and relied only on Earth for technical products, spare parts and the luxuries of life. Plans were already well developed for the construction of Altai 2, which would take another five years to construct, if only the US Government committed the necessary funds.

Pat was half dozing and half-awake as the shuttle van sped across the surface of the Moon, returning them to Altai. For once she felt weary but could now see the light at the end of the tunnel and was even starting to think about possibly returning to Earth permanently and let someone else have the responsibility for Altai and Altai 2.

She desperately missed the green grass, the glorious red sunsets and going to the ocean and hearing the waves crashing on the beach. But such a return would take over 12 months in gravity-retraining, an intense exercise program and a myriad of pills before she could think of returning to the Earth's surface, but it would be worth it!

Pat was soundly asleep when she was jolted awake by the alarm on her emergency beeper, which was an exceedingly rare event these days. She immediately sat upright in her seat when she saw the message which appeared on the screen, 'No not now, it just can't be possible!' 'What's the matter boss?' enquired Jonsey. Whilst Otis still slept blissfully unaware. 'Contact Altai and tell them we are at Code Purple, get Frank to set up the necessary comms and people on standby and tell our driver Captain Wojinski to get us to Altai pronto!'

Jonsey knew not to ask unnecessary questions and got to work.

Pat continued to look down at her screen as it repeatedly flashed the message 'EEE.' At first, she hoped it was an error, but then her practical mind kicked into gear. She knew that all her staff would already be moving to the lower-level bunker within five minutes of the alert tone and given the shuttle's speed and bumpy ride they would be at Altai very soon.

Pat hoped that this was not some kind of sick drill by Earth to test their preparedness!

Meanwhile, as usual Otis remained blissfully sound asleep all the way back to Altai despite the bumps.

chapter 9

SAN FRANCISCO
(UNITED STATES)

Dr Henry Stolz was at the end of a long day of seeing patients. He could not remember a run of patients in such a short period of time. The last few weeks had been horrendous; perhaps it was just because he was getting old!

'Your 3:45pm appointment is waiting!' buzzed his receptionist with an exasperated tone to her voice.

'Thanks Sue,' and glancing down at his watch he was surprised that the time was already 6:40pm, 'It looks like we are going to have a nice midnight dinner again, almost as bad as yesterday! Please show them in.'

After another two hours of seeing patients and just when he thought the day was over, Sue buzzed through yet again. But this time it was not to announce the next patient, 'Doctor, I need to see you before you leave, as we have a, a situation.' Now Doctor Stolz knew that Sue was not one to panic, as she had been his receptionist now for over 25 years.

Sue walked into his office and stood in front of him

pointing to the appointment list on her Notepad, 'In all the time I have worked here, I have never seen this happen before. This afternoon, all I have done is make appointments. There have been over 40 calls and we have appointments until the end of the next month already. I think we are having a plague of Tinnitus!'

Dr Stolz had been coming to the same conclusion given the number of patients he had been seeing over the past few weeks. They were all coming in complaining of the same symptoms. At first, he just thought that his popularity as one of San Francisco's leader doctors in Tinnitus treatment had finally caught on. However, when he asked patients where they had heard about him, they all just said via the web or through referral from their local doctors. Something was happening, but he had no real idea what.

'Well Sue, let us close up and call it a day. Whilst many will not be happy, from now on only accept appointments from our current patients and don't take any new ones until further notice.'

'They're not going to like that!'

'Well, it just can't be helped.'

'That is fine Doctor, so long as you are going to be the one who handles all of the difficult callers who never take no for an answer!' said Sue and she then turned abruptly and strode out of his office without waiting for a reply.

Dr Stolz knew not to say anymore, he also knew that she would calm down, eventually. When he had finally packed up and walked wearily out from his office, he noticed that Sue had already left for the day without saying goodnight. He then locked the surgery door behind him and started his short walk home.

chapter 10

WASHINGTON DC
(UNITED STATES)

Dan Mars, Special Advisor to the President had gone to bed thinking about a whole raft of issues that needed to be raised with his boss in the early morning briefing session. His role was to make sure that there were no surprises for the President. But like all Presidents, he also usually wanted solutions as well. However, this time Dan had no idea about many of the recent strange occurrences nor if there was any link between them. It was 3am and he knew from experience that he was not going to get any more sleep tonight. So, he got up, made himself a hot chocolate, laced with a bit of whiskey, and sat down to read over the reports that were piled up on his desk. There was a detailed update from the Federal Department of Agriculture on the now international problem of dead bees and the projected impact on world food supplies. It was hard to believe but it seemed that many of the bees in the world were either dead or dying due to an alien species of mites. When he first read the report, he thought that the term *alien* had been used to indicate a new or unknown strain of domestic mite that was causing the problem. It was only when he read it a second time that he then understood that the report was really referring to an actual alien species, of non-terrestrial origin and source unknown. Attached to this report was a Top-Secret briefing by Emergency Management America (EMA) which had already begun contingency plans for the distribution of basic food via emergency outlets. EMA had also included some very frightening scenarios of potential food riots in most American cities, let alone the impact on the rest of the world. Given that bees accounted for 30 per cent of the world's food, the EMA report made horrific reading not just for America. This was sure going to make a good conversation topic for the President over her favourite sweet bagels at the breakfast briefing!

Dan then turned to the next report in the pile and smiled when he recognised his old alumni colleague, Pat Milner's name on the cover of the report. He quickly flipped through the contents, so he could update the President on Project Altai and then noticed that Pat was requesting again to begin construction of Altai 2. She only needed a cool $23 trillion! While the President loved Project Altai, Pat's timing for more money could not have come at a worse time. He was not looking forward to giving Pat the inevitable bad news!

Scanning through the remaining briefing papers he came across an unusual report from the Director of Public Health. He was reporting a 1000% increase in patients reporting with Tinnitus-like symptoms at Public Hospitals and general medical clinics over the past few weeks. Dan had to do a Google search on Tinnitus as whilst he had heard of it before, he was not sure what it really entailed, and he was sure that the President would be sure to ask him about it. The report went on to say that all of the reported cases appeared to be restricted to specific geographic locations which seemed unusual. Dan decided that it did not seem all that urgent and so he decided to refer it back to the Health Department to do more fieldwork. Due to terrorist protocols developed since 9/11, he also sent a copy to the FBI for their information. Well, that is one less report to worry about he thought, and as he reached for the last report in the pile the pink glow of sunrise was just appearing over the horizon.

The final report was from Professor Sally Stewart from Palomar Observatory in California and was marked URGENT. Her report referred to the observation of unusual marks on the surface of the sun and some high levels of radiation emissions. Dan chuckled to himself about getting to this report just now, as the sun glare through his office window was becoming too bright forcing him to move his position at his desk so that he could still read the report without being blinded by the glare of the sun. It was an overly complicated and technical report, typical of those the President had received previously from Professor Stewart. They always contained complex equations with little in the way of interpretation that anyone could understand. Dan scanned quickly through the lengthy document and found an obscure bookmark reference stating that the probability of a severe event was less than one per cent. Thank goodness he thought and decided to flick this one to NASA for their interpretation. If he remembered, he would also mention it to Pat next time he spoke to her and would send her a download copy of the report as well as a 'heads-up.'

Dan looked at his watch and realised that he was now running late. He dressed and grabbed his car keys and was quickly on his way to the White House.

chapter 11

SOUTH CHINA SEA

Almost at the same time as Dan Mars was having his morning coffee at the President's breakfast briefing, Commander Buck Beckmann on the nuclear submarine USS Obama was on-station just off the coast of China. Last night he had decided to check the new lights of Shanghai, which was under reconstruction, through the periscope, before settling back down on the ocean floor. His crew had been on duty for the past five weeks, with one more week to go before they swapped duty with the USS Nimrod. Then they would be on shore leave at the crew's favourite location, Hawaii.

Buck wondered what it must have been like in the days of the Cold War when hundreds of nuclear submarines patrolled the oceans, as now there was only the Nimrod and Obama. He also thought about his father who fought and died in what was called the Chinese Islands War which had occurred nearly 10 years ago. The Chinese Islands War had lasted just seven days when China decided to claim back all the islands off its coast, including two significant islands, namely Japan and Taiwan. Without any warning, nor intelligence alerts, China invaded both countries on the same day with over 5 million troops engaged. They quickly over-ran any opposition within three days through their overwhelming force. Despite United Nation's condemnation, China continued their expansion to fully control both countries and related islands of the heavily disputed South China Seas. Buck's father was on the USS Trump which was hit and sunk during the Battle of the Sea of Japan, which had also resulted in the destruction of the entire Chinese naval fleet.

To some observers, China appeared to have won this short war, as they still maintained some control over Taiwan and Hong Kong but were forced to totally relinquish and withdraw from Japan and all the China Sea islands outside their recognised territorial waters. However, the cost to China and the Chinese people proved to be exceedingly high. On the dawn of day seven, the Chinese lost the cities of Beijing and Shanghai, when the United States, endorsed by the Security Council of the United Nations (China had been expelled from the United Nations), simultaneously obliterated both cities with high yield hydrogen bombs. The death toll alone in these two cities was over 175 million people. At the end of the seventh day, the US were on the verge of dropping a third nuclear bomb on Nanjing when China surrendered, and peace was very quickly restored and thankfully it had held ever since.

At first, China lost most of its world trade and went back to being an extremely poor country with a totally decimated economy. However, since then peace had mostly returned to the planet and military forces around the world had significantly shrunk, including US forces. The United States maintained two operational nuclear submarines and as far as their intelligence agencies could ascertain, they were now the only country with any operational nuclear submarines. However, Buck and Strategic Command were not convinced, and that was why they were stationed off the coast of China. Over the past 10 years, China was again re-emerging as a world power and had invested heavily in space technology. They had also announced that they would begin mining on the moon and that they planned to establish a fully operational moon base within the next five years. Buck was happy for China to turn to space rather than building nuclear submarines. His only thought as he lowered the periscope was that he and his crew would be incredibly pleased when, yet another uneventful tour of duty was completed.

chapter 12

SAN FRANCISCO
(UNITED STATES)

It was finally the end of another week and Doctor Stolz was working late again. He was now convinced that his patients who were exhibiting classic Tinnitus symptoms, did not have the condition at all. He knew from years of experience that Tinnitus was a physical condition, experienced as noises or ringing in the ears or head, when no such external physical noise was present. Its severity was usually more related to stress or tiredness and exposure to loud noise, for example, noisy lawn mowers or chainsaws or exposure to loud music, through headphones or rock concerts. None of his recent patients reported any such circumstances and the condition appeared to come and go without any real pattern. It was only by accident that after reviewing the medical files that he noticed that many patients seemed to live in the same general location. And he was sure that this was not just a coincidence.

Upon packing up for the day, he grabbed several files and decided to go and have a look for himself. He drove his car and parked outside the Barklay Apartment building, which contained at least ten recent patients, with a further 18 patients located in the surrounding neighbourhood. At first, he looked around for a noisy factory perhaps or an electricity generator that may be the cause. But the neighbourhood appeared quiet with no major noise-causing development in sight.

It was still early evening as Dr Stolz walked up to the grand entry to the apartment building where there was an old-style revolving glass door which guests had to negotiate to enter the building. Once through the door he walked up to a shabby and poorly lit reception desk and standing behind the counter was a very tall smiling staff member.

Dr Stolz smiled back to the security officer, 'I'm a doctor, and I have several patients who are suffering from a hearing problem and rather strangely many of them either live in or near this building. I was wondering if you may be able to tell me if anything has happened in this building or changed in the area recently.'

'What kinda changes doc?' answered the security officer in a slow southern accent.

'Well, things like, for example, has someone been doing some building renovations, any demolition work of some kind, basically anything that may cause a lot of noise, that sort of thing.'

The receptionist paused to think, placing his hand on his face and rubbing his chin slowly and then replied, 'Nope, I've heard nothing like that.'

'Are you the only security officer, perhaps something happened when you were not at work?'

'Nope, not possible doc.'

'Why not, you can't be here all the time?' replied Dr Stolz.

'Well yep your right doc, there is another security officer who works here sometimes, but I live here, and I ain't heard anything like what you say.'

'That's a real pity,' responded Dr Stolz, 'I was sure there would be a logical solution to this problem, I still think that something strange is going on around here. I have ten clients who have been affected, all of them live in this building and I must find out why.'

The security officer just maintained a blank expression and realising that there was nothing further to be gained from talking to him, Dr Stolz turned and started to leave the building.

Just as he got to the revolving door, he heard the doorman yell out after him, 'Hey Doc, say we did have a new heatin unit put in the basement a couple of weeks ago. Is this what you may be looking for? I can show you if you would like to have a look?'

On hearing this, Dr Stolz did a sharp U-turn and he followed the tall security officer to a door leading to the basement.

'After you Dr Stolz.'

As Dr Stolz began walking down the stairs, he glanced quickly back at the security officer and asked, 'How on earth do you know my name?'

Before he was given an answer, he felt a strong shove in the middle of his back and he went tumbling down the steps and hitting the basement floor heavily. He was half lying on his back and intuitively knew by the unusual position of his right forearm that it was broken and his hip was starting to ache. He looked up as the security officer walked slowly down the last few steps and stood over him, no longer with a smile on his face.

Dr Stolz was just about to say something when he heard a loud buzzing in his ears. That is strange he thought. As a doctor he knew that he did not have concussion and as the noise grew louder, he was just surmising that perhaps for the first time in his life he may be suffering from the very complaint that most of his patients suffered from - Tinnitus. Just as he was beginning to feel genuine empathy for what his patients must live through every day, he realised the real source of the static noise. The cold dark eyes of the security officer told him everything.

Luckily for him the pain did not last long, but the darkness that surrounded him would last forever.

In the morning news there was a small item about an accident in a local apartment building. The police reported that there were no suspicious circumstances surrounding the death of Dr Stolz.

chapter 13

BENDIGO (AUSTRALIA)

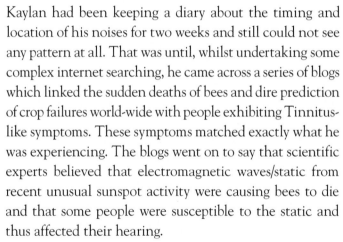

Kaylan had been keeping a diary about the timing and location of his noises for two weeks and still could not see any pattern at all. That was until, whilst undertaking some complex internet searching, he came across a series of blogs which linked the sudden deaths of bees and dire prediction of crop failures world-wide with people exhibiting Tinnitus-like symptoms. These symptoms matched exactly what he was experiencing. The blogs went on to say that scientific experts believed that electromagnetic waves/static from recent unusual sunspot activity were causing bees to die and that some people were susceptible to the static and thus affected their hearing.

So finally, he knew what was causing his problem, it was the static noise emitted from recent sunspots. No wonder he could not find a pattern! He could not wait to get home and tell his mother.

As usual he found his mother waiting for him on the front steps, 'Hi darling, how was school today?'

'Fine mum, but I need to talk to you about the noises - I

have found the cause! You know about the recent sunspot activity, they say that the sun is producing electromagnetic static, and that some people's hearing is affected. The same noises that I can hear. I'm sure!'

His mother, with a wry smile on her face said, 'So you think this static noise you are hearing is caused by the sun?

Even before Kaylan could nod in agreement, his mother continued, 'Kaylan, I thought you were so much smarter than that!'

And at that point she just stood up, turned around and walked inside without saying another word.

Kaylan stood dumbfounded; his mother had never spoken to him that way before. But how could he, and the world, get it so wrong?

chapter 14

NEWCASTLE (AUSTRALIA)

Dr Hawthorne had watched with trepidation the growing media circus and unfolding crisis of dead bees worldwide and he knew all too well the catastrophic effect it was going to have on food production. He had been viewing, but not participating in social media's increasing use of the term *Vegemite*. He knew that it was all related to the sample of mites that he had sent to Dr Reid.

He knew at once that Dr Reid's initial strange response was totally out of character. They knew each other too well. Nothing had arrived by email from Dr Reid as promised and for days he tried to contact him without success. He knew something was wrong, very wrong.

It was almost a week later that Dr Hawthorne received a call from another colleague wondering if he had heard about Dr Reid's death and if he was going to attend the funeral. Recovering from his initial shock, he was told about his death at the hands of an unidentified burglar, who was still on the run from police.

Fortunately, the funeral had been delayed because of

the police investigation and autopsy so that Dr Hawthorne would be able to attend. He also hoped that perhaps some other colleagues would be there and they may be able to shed some light on what happened to Dr Reid and provide some answers to his last conversation with his friend.

chapᴛꞒꝛ 15

BENDIGO (AUSTRALIA)

Kaylan was having another sleepless night. He tried to understand his mother's strange response and began to come up with stranger and wilder ideas as to what may be causing the noises. He decided to dismiss the connection with bees as just a coincidence. On reflection, Kaylan thought that the noises seemed to be more related to particular people, but he had no idea who or why.

Each time he was about to fall asleep, a growing sense of impending danger intruded into his thoughts. He was just about to get out of bed being driven by an even stronger sense of danger when his mother burst into his bedroom.

'Good you're awake, we are in danger and have to leave now! Get dressed; I have already packed what we need into the car.'

Once in the car, his mother drove without saying anything further. And Kaylan knew, without being told, that they were really in danger and heading towards a safe place. But where, he did not know.

They drove back into the City of Bendigo and Kaylan immediately recognised the entrance to the Central Deborah Gold Mine facility. He had visited the mine in a school excursion.

'What are we doing here mum? They don't open up for hours yet.'

Kaylan's mother drove through the open gates of the Deborah Gold Mine and parked right at the entry to the mine portal. Kaylan was surprised to see that there was someone waiting for them at the mine entry. The stranger warmly welcomed his mother, as if he knew her, and directed them to the lift. After a slow and noisy descent, they arrived at the bottom of the main shaft, a depth of 412 metres, if the large sign at the lift exit was accurate. The stranger then pointed in the direction of a long and dimly lit tunnel, which they walked down for a further 100 metres until they arrived at a heavy fire safety door.

Once through the door, the stranger closed it with an almighty clang which seemed to reverberate forever in the mine and loudly announced, 'You're the last ones here; all the others are here already.'

There in front of them were 14 other people, all sitting quietly in a large, cavernous space. Kaylan had never seen these people before, however his mother seemed to need no introductions and was welcomed as if she was a long-lost friend!

'Who are these people?' asked Kaylan.

chapter 16

MELBOURNE (AUSTRALIA)

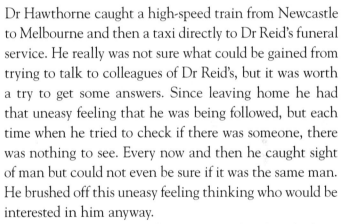

Dr Hawthorne caught a high-speed train from Newcastle to Melbourne and then a taxi directly to Dr Reid's funeral service. He really was not sure what could be gained from trying to talk to colleagues of Dr Reid's, but it was worth a try to get some answers. Since leaving home he had that uneasy feeling that he was being followed, but each time when he tried to check if there was someone, there was nothing to see. Every now and then he caught sight of man but could not even be sure if it was the same man. He brushed off this uneasy feeling thinking who would be interested in him anyway.

The taxi finally arrived outside the Church with about 30 minutes to spare before the service began. Initially he was totally surprised by the mass of people surrounding the chapel. He knew Dr Reid was well regarded, but surely, he was not that well known. And he was not an international personality as one would think by the size of the media pack, with reporters and television crews everywhere.

He emerged from the taxi and walked slowly towards

the chapel trying to seek out any familiar faces. Not seeing anyone he knew, he decided to go directly to the chapel.

He was about the enter the chapel when a loud voice boomed, 'Dr Hawthorne, Dr Hawthorne, a question if you please?' Like a hungry pack of wolves, the press, whom up to now had totally ignored him, all turned in unison and rushed forward. Before he knew it, he had microphones and cameras all pointed in his direction.

'Dr Hawthorne, how well did you know the late Dr Reid?'

'Ah well, we both went to school together and we have remained friends ever since.'

'What prompted you to send a sample of dead bees to Dr Reid?' This question completely took Dr Hawthorne by surprise, as he thought that whilst a few people knew of his connection with Dr Reid, nobody would know about the samples. But even before he could respond, another anonymous questioner followed up with a further question, 'You are also friends with Bill Bishop, so what are you hiding Dr Hawthorne?'

At first, he was completely confused and began by saying, 'Bill, oh yes, we are also good friends.'

'What are you hiding Dr Hawthorne?'

'I'm not trying to hide anything, what are you trying to suggest?' Dr Hawthorne now felt trapped and was looking for a way out of this mayhem before any more questions were asked.

'Well, how do you explain that Dr Reid was killed, Dr McKewan in UK also died under suspicious circumstances and now Bill Bishop is now missing. These are all friends of yours. They were investigating the cause of bees dying world-wide. And now that you have come out of hiding, what do you have to say Dr Hawthorne. We want answers and you seem to be right in the middle of this mess.'

Dr Hawthorne had never had to face the media before and they were being particularly aggressive. He had nowhere to hide so he decided the best approach was just to say what he knew, or at least what he thought he knew.

'Well Dr Hawthorne, when are we going to get some answers?' pressed another reporter even more aggressively.

He collected his thoughts, took a deep breath and with his voice still quivering, 'Firstly, I was not aware that Dr McKewan was dead and that Bill Bishop is missing. Bill and I both live in Newcastle and share a beer on occasions. Unfortunately, I have not seen him nor talked to him since he gave me the sample of dead bees.'

'Why did he give them to you, bees are a little out of your league aren't they, given that you are a vet?'

'Well Bill came to me after many of his members were reporting the deaths of their beehives in large numbers and he didn't know where to go next. He thought I may have a contact or an idea of whom else to go to for help.'

'What did you both decide to do?'

'Bill told me he thought that there was a new strain of mites that he and his members had found on the skin of the bees were responsible for their deaths. He asked me if I knew anyone who could do an independent laboratory test on the bees. For the record, Bill had profoundly serious concerns that government labs were giving him the run around and deliberately delaying and even falsifying the results for some unknown reason. As a result, I was happy to forward the sample of bees to Dr Reid for testing.'

Now feeling a little more composed, Dr Hawthorne continued, 'And I just want to add that I hope that Bill will turn up safe and well and that his disappearance it is not connected with the deaths of Dr Reid or Dr McKewan.'

'So, you sent the sample to Dr Reid, what happened next?'

'Ah yes, well at first there was some delay and I could not get onto Dr Reid. When I finally did, he informed me that the sample mites were just a more virulent strain of a common Asian Vampire Mite and nothing to worry about.'

'When did this conversation take place?'

'It was only after hearing the news of Dr Reid's death in the media, I subsequently realised that he must have been murdered shortly after my call.'

'So, you were probably the last person to talk to Dr Reid alive?'

'Well yes, that would seem correct.'

'So, the mites have nothing to do with dying bees?'

'No, I didn't say that.'

'Oh, come off it doc, we just heard you say that the mites were nothing to worry about, to use your words!'

'No, I said that Dr Reid said that! Even at the time I did not believe what Dr Reid had said, I am sure that he was under duress to say that.'

'How can you be so sure?'

'Well at the time, he told me that affected beehives would die in two or three months, when in all previous conversations he was aware that whole beehives were dying within days, not months. It just did not add up.

It did not add up then and it doesn't add up now. I am convinced that the sample was much more than just a different species of mite. It is clear, and I think that both Bill and Doctors Reid and McKewan knew, that the mites and the death of bees were part of a much bigger issue. One that the Government would rather keep quiet. In my conversations with Dr Reid and Dr McKewan, they used the term *Vegemites*, and from checking other communications from similar experts around the world, they too have been talking about *Vegemites*. And I also believe, no, I strongly believe, Dr Reid, and now most likely Dr McKewan were killed for what he found out about these so-called *Vegemites*.'

Pandemonium broke out and it was impossible to hear any single question, but finally a couple of reporters clearly called out above the others, 'What's a *Vegemite*?'

'I think it was either Dr Reid's or a colleague's code for a new strain of mite. A mite with a totally different strain of DNA. We are only now becoming aware that this new mite is effectively killing every species of bee on the planet. If reports are correct, nearly the whole world's bee population is either dead or dying. This will have a catastrophic effect on our food supplies. This is what I believe the authorities have been trying to keep from the public. However, I think it will get worse.'

'How so?'

'What I really believe is that Dr Reid and some of his colleagues were more concerned regarding this new strain of mites and what impact they may have on other species. On the train down this morning, I saw some disturbing news reports coming out of Europe which talked about sudden and strange deaths of chickens and birds.'

'What's that got to do with the mites?'

'I think that the mites, these *Vegemites*, may have mutated and have now moved from one species to another.'

'But where have these *Vegemites* come from?

'I am sure that Dr Reid had some ideas as well and that is why he was killed. But I can only guess. The *Vegemites* could be a mutation from an existing species or they may be completely foreign to the Earth. But either way, we are facing a very clever killer mite. Who knows where it may end up?'

'If it is from outer space, how did it get here?'

'That is the six-billion-dollar question that you should be asking the government. Perhaps somehow, they arrived from space via a meteor's water vapour trail or space dust, who knows?'

'How can something so small prove to be so deadly?'

'That's a particularly good question. I am reminded of a famous book written by H G Wells, called the 'War of the Worlds. Only this time, instead of one of our germs infecting the invading aliens and killing them, perhaps an invading alien germ is killing first our bees and then other animals and may in the end kill us as well!'

On that point Dr Hawthorne broke off the interview and strode into the chapel leaving a gaggle of reporters screaming more questions after him.

Once inside, Dr Hawthorne found a chair at the end of a pew and tried to calm down. The funeral service was short and just as Dr Hawthorne was thinking about how to get out of the chapel and away from any reporters, two large shadows appeared over him, 'This is Mr Grey and I am Mr Brown, please come this way Dr Hawthorne. We will take you away from all of the reporters outside, as we think you have done enough damage for one day!'

chapter 17

SAN FRANCISCO
(UNITED STATES)

Earlier that same day, the smiling security officer at the Barklay Apartment Building was quite pleased with himself. He had been able to easily steal a minibus and had dutifully picked up seven other members of 'the family' and they were now heading towards the safest place he knew, a place he and another member of the 'family' had picked out in preparation for an emergency.

When they arrived at the Sausalito Sewerage Treatment Plant, the smiling security officer swiped a security pass and they all headed for the main control room, 30 floors underground. Here they were warmly met by another man wearing a lab coat and shown inside.

They all knew that something horrible was about to happen and that they may have a long time to wait before being rescued. However, the huge piles of food and water stacked along the walls reassured them that they were now safe.

chapter 18

KOPANANG (SOUTH AFRICA)

Meanwhile in a South African gold mine in Kopanang, a group of 40 miners and staff were preparing to conduct an emergency safety drill, under the direction of Dr Walter Basson, the Chief Medical Officer of the mine.

Dr Basson had become increasingly concerned that the authorities seemed to be getting closer and closer to chasing them down. It appeared that the South African Secret Service (SASS) and the CIA were working together and were checking the identities of everyone in Kopanang. It would be only a matter of time before they came to the mine. Whilst their identities had been sufficient for the mining company, they would not pass the scrutiny of professionals.

Dr Basson decided that the time had come. As he entered No.2 Elevator, his hand clasped a remote control and he pressed the red button once. This armed the warhead. As other miners began to fill the elevator, he held down the red button for a further five seconds. This activated the retrorockets sending the warhead on its intended trajectory. Well, the die is now well and truly cast, he thought to himself.

As the mine elevator began its noisy descent into the mine, he hoped that whilst he could not directly communicate to the others, that they would sense the warning and take the necessary precautions as planned.

chapter 19

PALOMAR OBSERVATORY
CALIFORNIA (UNITED STATES)

It was not a normal day at the world-famous Palomar Observatory in California. Professor Sally Stewart had just finished working with the last group of fresh-faced research students for the day and was anxious to get back to watching the sun in all its glory. She was totally excited as she believed that she was possibly witnessing a potential solar-burst event that may only occur every 100 million years. What a privilege! Placing the telescope image on the large viewing screen she could now clearly see the unusual sunspot activity that she and her colleagues around the world had been witnessing over the past few weeks.

Being such an unusual event, she submitted her Priority Status Report directly to the President of the United States, as required by protocol. She was totally dismayed when she had been informed by Dan Mars, the President's adviser, that her report had been forwarded to NASA for further comment. What on earth would those clowns at NASA know anyway, she thought!

The sun was now beginning to set, so Sally began to complete the hand-over procedures to other observatories. Just as she was about to switch-off she noticed what appeared to be the sun blinking! A small dark spot rapidly expanded to envelop almost forty percent of the visible surface of the sun, and then it exploded in a fiery mass. Sally had observed similar solar events before, in other galaxies, but this time it was on our Sun, in our solar system!

'Oh my god, I don't believe what I just saw!'

She immediately contacted colleagues at Parkes Observatory in Australia, who were now online, 'Are you guys seeing this?'

'Yes, but we don't believe it. The sun's going supernova and turning into a Neutron Star! But it can't be happening, can it?'

'There's no doubt, I'm going to have to call this one quickly, do you concur?'

'Yes, we do, and god help us all!'

Sally immediately reached for her special mobile phone which linked her directly to Crystal Peak, the United States Government Military Communications Centre. She sent the message that she hoped that she would never have to send. Her fingers were shaking as she typed in her security code followed by the letters 'EEE[5]'. She was only one of five people on the entire planet with the power to send such a message!

Sally then sat in awe looking at monitors which showed vision from several observatories around the world depicting an explosive ball of fire coming from the sun. She watched in horror as the tendril of fire rapidly reached and consumed Venus in a ring of fire. She knew then that she was witnessing the death of the solar system. Earth only had hours of life left and nothing could be done, other than the message she had just sent which may just save a handful of people.

chapter 20

SOUTH CHINA SEA

The USS Obama had been running silent for the past couple of days when their solitary routine was rudely interrupted by a scrambled priority message from Crystal Peak.

Buck read the code 'EEE' and immediately gave the order for battle stations and to make maximum depth. The coded message automatically triggered Defcon Level 1 and as such they were now preparing for an immediate launch of the birds.

'Dive, dive, dive!' he ordered as the klaxon bells sounded throughout the submarine.

Buck's first thought was, 'What has China done now!'

chapter 21

SKYLAB XIII

Commander Neil Lavarche along with his small crew comprising Corporals Sue Jones and Jenny Fitzgibbon had been stationed on Skylab for nearly 12 months and were due for rotation soon. He loved working in space and had thoroughly enjoyed his work and the role that Skylab played in new research and monitoring satellites.

Orbiting the Earth every day were tens of thousands of communication satellites and their job, and NASA's, was to track and monitor them all and undertake necessary repairs. There were also many secret military satellites which were usually found by accident, as no-one was going to admit that they even existed.

Unfortunately, they often came across incredibly old satellites which were launched between the cold war and the Chinese Island war, many with nuclear weapons. Some could take months to repair; many were just recycled for scrap and a few were sent on a trajectory to the sun for safe disposal.

NASA and Skylab were given this role under United

Nations Space Charter 10/2042/E125. This UN edict only came as a result when an old and secret USSR satellite fell to Earth with armed nuclear warheads. It had crashed in downtown Jakarta, vaporising 12 million people and injuring another 20 million. Russia denied all knowledge of the satellite, despite the evidence, but did settle with Indonesia with significant on-going financial support.

Skylab's role was to ensure that it did not happen again.

Simultaneously as the USS Obama received the EEE Coded signal, so did Skylab XIII. Commander Lavarche was not aware that an EEE code even existed, let alone also being advised of Defcon 1. He had to refer to Skylab's bible of procedures to see what they meant!

'What in hell is happening down there now?' he said to Corporal Jones who was sitting beside him, 'we'd better seek confirmation from NASA on this one!'

Before they could contact NASA, the answer became obvious. They were currently orbiting on the dark side of the Earth and looking out of their view ports they could see the night lights of cities and town as a strange glow appeared on the horizon of the Earth that just got brighter and brighter. It was if someone turned a bright light on the other side of the Earth as the tendrils of red-hot light shot out from the Earth and into space beyond.

Then Skylab's power went off as the circuit-breakers tripped.

The crew watched as the red glow seemingly smashed into the atmosphere. As luck would have it, their orbit now followed directly behind the solar storm and pulses, and while they were safe, they were witnessing the destruction of the planet. All the land areas were either burning white hot or completely blackened. They did not need to use the thermal images to ascertain areas of heat on the surface, they could see them. The atmosphere or what was left was crystal clear as all the moisture in the air had been evaporated. It was also unlikely that any oxygen would remain as well. Nothing at or near the surface would be able to survive. The land areas had suffered from firestorms of the worst kind.

Given the current positions of the Moon it was highly likely that Altai base on the moon would be okay. Their priority was to get power back online and reboot all of their systems so that they could restore communications.

chapter 22

ALTAI (MOON)

Pat and the drilling team from the mine went straight down into the lower level which contained the communication centre and emergency bunker.

As Pat emerged from the lift, she was pleased to see that everyone appeared calm and were congregated in the bunker. She could immediately sense the added tension in the room as this was the first time they had gone to Code Purple, the highest alert level, apart from the mandatory monthly drills.

And now she knew that this was not a drill, as she received the second confirmation EEE Code and the Defcon 1 alert as she was coming down in the lift.

Under EEE protocols her first task was to go straight to the secure communications room and to receive the secure package of information from Earth. Altai was the emergency backup site for all the Earth's core financial and security agency data.

All the Moonies who saw Pat enter the bunker and

watch her go immediately to the 'secret' comms room now also knew for certain that this was no ordinary drill.

Pat settled down at the desk and punched in her security code on the computer and waited. She quickly scanned Altai's mainframe computer system which was running hot with file downloads. Whilst she waited for the first voice message to come through her annoyance level rose as these types of direct conversations with Earth always felt so truncated, due to the 1.3 second sound delay.

Pat was surprised to see the face of Dan Mars come up on her monitor, as she had been expecting one of the NASA chiefs. Now Pat knew that this was serious, with Dan being the second most important man in the world. Whilst it had only been 6 months since they had last talked via video screen, she noticed immediately that Dan looked 20 years older as his face was puffy and grey, 'Hi Pat, sorry that I do not have time for pleasantries and given the infernal time delay I will brief you first in full with no interruptions, and then get you to ask all your questions in one go. Then I will reply if I can as time is not on our side. I assume you have commenced recording as per Earth Extinction Event (EEE) protocols and will pause now just in case.'

So, after a briefest of pauses, Dan continued, 'as of 5:10am Washington time, that's exactly 12 minutes ago, NASA's Advanced Composition Explorer (ACE) which provides us with the most accurate indicator of incoming space weather, detected a major event on the surface of the sun. Staff at the Palomar Observatory in California made the EEE alert virtually at the same time. We had seen similar solar flare eruptions before, but nothing compared to the size and scale of what we are witnessing now. We have no idea what may have caused the eruption on the sun, although our observatories have been witnessing unusual activity for the past few weeks. We estimate that the first solar pulse will hit the Earth in around 10 minutes and will be followed by several secondary pulses over the next 12 – 18 hours. The only similar situation that we are aware of is the pulse which struck the Earth back in 1859. This event caused the failure of telegraph systems all over Europe and North America. Auroras were reportedly seen as far south as Florida. It was called the *Carrington Event*[6]. These pulses consist of powerful plasma balls blasting out from the surface of the sun and depending upon their intensity could wipe out our modern electricity grids, transformers, computers and satellites. At this stage we are unsure of the intensity of the pulses or the heat being generated. We do know that the Horizon IV Satellite which orbits Venus went off the air immediately upon being hit by the pulse when all its systems were fried. So, we are expecting it to be extremely powerful. The worst-case scenario, and we have many experts who concur, indicate that we are possibly experiencing a Supernova. All the scientists never thought that this was even possible. We could be seeing the death of the Sun, three billion years too early! If it is, then it is goodbye to life as we know it on Earth! We are currently evacuating the White House and if I lose you, it will be because I am already in the lift heading for PEOC, the President's Emergency Operations Centre[7] under the East Wing. We have issued orders shutting down all US power and electronic systems at T-minus 2 minutes, that's 5:15am Washington time. Once the solar storm has passed, we will then begin to power up what is left. Now as for Altai it appears you may be saved from most of this given the current relative positions of the moon, the Earth and the Sun. NASA has projected that for the next 17 hours, due to a lucky coincidence, the Moon which will traverse between the Sun and the Earth and the position of Altai facing the Earth during this period. In addition, your bunker is designed for just this type of event given your normal exposure to solar events. So, we think that you should be able to hunker-down and weather this one out. You will be hit by the solar pulses and some peripheral impact from the storm, depending upon how long it lasts, but nothing like what we may get back here on Earth! The President has ordered Defcon 1 status as a normal protocol in such an event. We have placed an Earth-wide alert on all forms of communications for people to take shelter as soon as they can. We anticipate two separate components to the solar storm. Firstly, there will be a series of electromagnetic solar pulses which will hit and instantly knock out all electronic equipment and signals. This will then be followed by the searing heat from the solar storm which appears to be in several different waves or varying intensities. Given the current planetary positions, the solar pulses and blasts will hit Europe, America and Asia.

It is now T-Minus eight minutes, now any questions?"

Pat knew that she had to be quick to get a reply, so as soon as Dan had mentioned the time, she had reset her digital timer and it glowed 7:53 and watched it as it quickly counted down.

'OK Dan, I have a few questions. How likely is that worst case scenario? What assets have you been able to launch or move to safe orbits? I already know from our servers that you are dumping all the usual stuff and fail-safe files to us as we speak. Can you also send me everything for Project Levitation, as I'm afraid we may need it! There are many more questions, but no time, and I am sure you have enough to do.'

While Pat was waiting for the reply, she summoned her Deputy Commander Frank Setaro and arranged for him to begin screening Dan's message to all staff who were waiting anxiously in the hub to let them know what was going on. She also ordered a communication shutdown on all non-essential systems on Altai. From previous drills, Pat knew that the base should be safe, once all precautions were taken, as her team knew the risks posed by solar storms.

After what seemed an eternity and the clock breaking through the 4:00 barrier, Dan appeared back on screen, and this time he was seated at a different desk.

'Thanks Pat, first, worst case... we really don't know, we hope that the Sun is not really going Supernova, but even so there is a high risk this could still be an Earth Extinction Event. Given early predictive readings from observatories and expert comment, we estimate that at least two-thirds of the world's population are likely to be killed and most, if not all, electronic and electrical systems will be destroyed. Basically, we have a high probability of going back to the stone-age. Secondly NASA has already re-tasked a couple of communication satellites so that we may be able to keep your communication lines open. We have alerted Skylab XIII, and fortunately like Altai, their current orbit will have the shelter of the Earth and they will be able to maintain their current protected position for the duration of the storm. We are already too late for NASA to launch anything so what supplies you already have will have to do. Who knows when you may get further supplies? And yes, good idea, I will send you everything we have on Project Levitation. I suppose it no longer matters but the President did not approve the funding allocation for Altai 2 and it has been postponed indefinitely, sorry! And one more thing, on the authority of the President, I have also sent to you a highly sensitive packet for your eyes only on the encrypted secure link. You will only need to open this message if the worst-case scenario occurs and you are unable to reconnect with Earth. If I can, I will call you after this is all over. Good luck and god be with you and god bless America, over.' The screen then went dead and Pat wondered if this may be the last ever communication from Earth.

Pat walked into the hub just as her crew were listening to the finish of Dan's initial briefing and the mood of the room was understandably subdued. All eyes turned to Pat, 'Thank you everyone. I appreciate how you have all responded to this emerging crisis. I was able to ask the President's Special Advisor a few extra questions before communications were cut. As you are aware I do not have to emphasise the seriousness of this threat. Worst-case scenario is catastrophic and is an e-cubed situation. Sorry for the code, an Earth Extinction Event. This is a potential catastrophe almost beyond comprehension. It appears that the solar storm and pulses will possibly hit most surface areas of the Earth with a resultant extreme loss of life. The damage to all electrical and electronic systems could take decades to repair. That is if they can be repaired at all! NASA have tried to re-task a couple of satellites into safer orbits to hopefully allow continued communications for us with Earth, once re-established. They were unable to launch any shuttles with supplies, so as of now we are all on rations, until we know the severity and duration of this event. Some good news, our old friends at Skylab XIII appear to be the only asset which by chance, like us, is in a protected position relative to the Sun.'

Pat was about to continue when she noticed that everyone's eyes had moved from focussing on her to staring at the main monitors immediately behind and above her. On the monitor they could see the Earth clearly in the centre of the screen and then a red glow appeared from the outer edges of the screen and then it completely encompassed the whole screen.

'Shit!' said Pat, suddenly realising that she had said that aloud, the solar flare must have been travelling almost at the speed of light and would hit the Earth almost as at the same time as the pulses.

It was only a matter of milliseconds when Altai's surface cameras failed, and all the monitors went blank and then the lights went out. They were in total darkness until the emergency lighting kicked in.

Frank then announced in a poor attempt of humour, 'Ah I'm sorry folks, that's the end of our coverage for tonight.'

The solar pulse had fried all their sensors on the surface. The surface temperature spiked at above 250 degrees centigrade and the radiation peaked at over 100,000 times the maximum safe radiations levels. To no one and yet everyone in the room heard, Pat moaned, 'Oh my god if this is anything like what is going to hit the Earth, god help them.'

After a few stifled sobs, the whole bunker went deathly silent.

chapter 23

WASHINGTON DC
(UNITED STATES)

Dan Mars, the President and her personal entourage, the Secretary of State, Leaders of the Senate and other key military support staff made their way down to the PEOC. While other staff and agencies headed for their own bunkers, many of which were established during the Cold War. PEOC in theory was where they were meant to be able to control the country and all communications. Alerts regarding the solar storm and pulses had gone out on all channels to the military and Dan had contacted Altai, and whilst NASA controlled Skylab XIII, he also patched them in on one of his messages. Altai housed the US information fail safe where all records from Wall Street, core business, Universities and Government were sent in a high-speed download program for safe keeping, just for an eventuality like this. No one had ever expected to use it! Everyone also expected that the President would be the first to know, however this was rarely the case. Whilst information was being relayed constantly into the

White House, it went through many hands first! By the time it got to the President it had usually already been on cable news services moments before, which infuriated the President. So, for most of them in PEOC, along with Dan, they did not know any more and were just waiting like everyone else for the solar storm to run its course.

From previous expert advice, they knew that the solar storm and pulses would continue for many hours yet.

Like the rest of the world, they were totally blind as there were no communications anywhere as all satellites and ground-based communication facilities had been knocked out by the solar storm.

chapter 24

SAN FRANCISCO
(UNITED STATES)

It was late morning when Sue arrived and unlocked the surgery door. She had been informed of the death of her boss Dr Stolz over breakfast when she saw it in the morning news report. She was at a total loss as to why Dr Stolz had gone to that part of town and to that apartment building after work, as it was in the opposite direction to his home. The rest of the news was equally depressing regarding unconfirmed reports of a solar storm that may affect mobile phones and the ongoing report of bees dying and impact on food. They were already reporting panic buying in supermarkets nation-wide!

Even though it was all so depressing and still recovering from the shock, she decided that she must go into the office to cancel all the upcoming patient appointments and then find out what Dr Stolz's family wanted to do with the office.

As soon as she opened the office door she walked into chaos. All her neat files were strewn across the floor. Every filing cabinet draw was open, and the contents emptied. She collapsed in the middle of the floor, crying. As she started to calm herself down, she thought that his death might not be an accident after all. She was just about to call the police when the room was filled with an orange glow, then came the searing heat.

She stared in amazement as the room self-ignited before her eyes in a ball of flames.

chapter 25

MELBOURNE (AUSTRALIA)

Dr Hawthorne reluctantly climbed into the back seat of the car with these two strangers.

'Where are you taking me. I do have a right to know!'

All he got was silence as they drove out of Melbourne. He then thought of all the television shows he had seen and began wondering if he was being driven to some remote place, only to be killed and dumped. Or were they taking him somewhere to be questioned, or even tortured? He looked around for a door handle, only to find there was none. Now he was worried.

Were these the same people who killed Dr Reid? Just as he was about to really think about how to escape, Mr Grey turned up the radio. 'Emergency communication channels will operate, and you will need to use battery-operated radios. Further announcements will be made on emergency channel 99. We are now shutting down transmission, God bless Australia.'

'What on earth was that all about?' said Mr Brown

who was driving with one hand on the steering wheel and the other hand hanging out of the window.

Just at that point Dr Hawthorne looked outside to see the sky turn a bright orange. Then came the searing heat, followed by the smell of burning flesh, his burning flesh!

His scream and those of Mr Grey and Mr Brown were only cut off by two related events. Firstly, by their bodies being microwaved, and secondly the car crashing into a tree and exploding as the soaring heat ignited the petrol tank.

chapter 26

BENDIGO (AUSTRALIA)

Kaylan had decided that this was the strangest group of people he had ever met. Stranger still, he was the youngest in the tunnel. The group were all crowded around a small radio and listening intently, so Kaylan and his mother sat down as well, just as an announcement came on.

Even the radio announcer sounded nervous and began reading from a prepared script, 'The Federal Government has just released an urgent bulletin to go out on all communication channels. A severe solar storm will impact most areas of the Earth over the next 12-18 hours. All Australians are advised to immediately seek shelter, preferably underground, and not to venture out into the open until safe to do so. All power supplies will be switched off to minimise possible burning out of cables and electrical equipment because of the solar pulses. Emergency communication channels will operate; however, they will need to be operated by batteries until it is safe to resume normal power supplies. Further announcements will be made on emergency channel 99. All communication channels will be repeating this message until normal transmissions are able to be resumed. If you know of someone who may not have access to communication or will require assistance to move into shelter, please assist. Where possible all building operators have been requested to open basements and all other underground facilities. Under no circumstance should you be out in the open during the solar storm and we request that you move to such underground spaces immediately. All airline traffic has been grounded until further notice.' Then the announcement continued as before, 'The Federal Government......'

As Kaylan was listening to the announcement, he was sure that these strange people were still talking to each other by their facial expressions, but there was not a sound and their lips did not move. There was no doubt that the noise in his head now had to be related to them in some way as he was nearly being deafened by it! But the noise itself did not make any sense. He just sat in amazement in a room of total silence – but his head full of noise.

Every now and then his mother pointed to him when *talking without saying any words* to her new, long-lost friends!

chapter 27

WASHINGTON DC
(UNITED STATES)

The President's Secret Service Team had gone up in the lift to reach the surface and more importantly to try reconnecting the antenna as it seemed to have been knocked out by the solar storm. After a couple of minutes, they reported back to say that the lift had stopped about half-way up as the shaft was blocked by debris.

This was not received well by the President as it meant that the damage on the surface was far worse than everyone had anticipated. They all knew that they just had to break through to re-gain communications with the rest of the world. No one, especially Dan, wanted this presidential sanctuary to turn into a burial site.

They could hear a lot of noise coming from the lift well as the agents were obviously trying to clear it, but it was the *bagman* who alerted everyone in the bunker to another noise, one that was being emitted from the 'bag'. On opening the bag, he said, 'Ah Madam President, I think we may have just launched a nuclear attack.'

'What do you mean we just ordered the launch of our nukes; we can't even order a take-away. Why didn't you tell us before that you could talk to the outside world!'

'Well, you see Madam President, we can't actually communicate, but the system was designed to operate in fail-safe situations and uses a grid of sensors around the US which light up when a launch has been made or there is an incoming nuke. As you can see the whole panel has lit up. We have multiple missile launches and multiple inbound as well. It appears that the storm or pulses might have activated the silos, or someone has taken advantage of the solar storm and initiated a nuclear war. Being on Defcon 1, our missiles were all armed and ready to go.'

'There must be something that we can do?'

'Sorry Madam President, not from here, we can only hope that Crystal Peak is still functioning.'

Dan just shook his head, wondering what else could go wrong. Unfortunately, they were all about to find out.

Without any warning the bunker was hit by a tremendous shockwave and whilst the structure was sound, the vibrations caused a horrible concussion to every living person inside. Everyone in the bunker was either killed instantly or died very soon after.

Whilst the bunker was meant to be safe, even in the case of a direct nuclear hit on the White House, they did not know about two important factors. Firstly, that the Chinese had significantly improved their bunker-buster technology so that nuclear warheads were able to penetrate deeper into the surface before detonating. Secondly and more importantly, unfortunately for the White House, it had been an unusually wet season and the soft sedimentary deposits surrounding the bunker held a very high-water content. The shock waves from the nuclear explosion were able to hit the bunker with tremendous force and the bunker itself rattled around as it had no stable footings. This caused the extreme vibrations inside.

chapter 28

SKYLAB XIII

Just as they thought it could not get any worse, they witnessed the beginning of thousands of white flashes and trails from rockets reaching the upper atmosphere and falling back into cities that were already white hot.

It was Captain Lavarche who provided the explanation for his crew, 'Somehow all of the nuclear weapons fail safe systems must have been automatically triggered by the pulses, the heat or others simply being on an automatic response circuit if fired upon. Something I remember hearing about in training, I think it was called the *Cerberus Protocol*[8]. This allowed the nukes to respond automatically on Defcon 1 if a silo detected the proximity of an incoming missile.'

Corporal Jones, Captain Lavarche's communications officer, had been constantly scanning all frequencies for any signals when she was suddenly able to pick up a military frequency, 'Captain, I think I have something, it could be a transmission from a US submarine in the Pacific.'

'Patch it through.'

'I repeat, this is the USS Obama on station at Defcon 1. We have detected multiple nuclear missile launches. We have lost contact with Crystal Peak, repeat we have lost contact with Crystal Peak, is anyone out there?'

'USS Obama, USS Obama, we read you loud and clear. This is Captain Lavarche on Skylab XIII, do you copy, over?'

'Skylab, Skylab are we happy to hear from you! This is Commander Buck Beckmann. Are you able to connect us or provide status, over?'

Captain Lavarche reported on the status as far as they could see from Skylab, including the missile launches. They both agreed to wait for further updates and stay in contact when Skylab's orbit allowed, as all other satellite communications were down, most likely permanently! So, Skylab could only communicate with the USS Obama when in range, without the Earth getting in the way and blocking the communications.

The deadly fireworks continued to flash across the globe for another two hours and then thankfully finally stopped.

chapter 29

ALTAI (MOON)

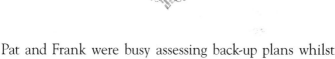

Pat and Frank were busy assessing back-up plans whilst emergency teams were working throughout the bunker and on the surface trying to get all their systems back online. Altai had been saved from the worst of the carnage experienced on Earth as the shadow affect had protected them from most of the severe solar storm heat and the electromagnetic pulses. All their greenhouses were intact, but all electronic instruments on the surface and on the top level of Altai had been severely affected. They had been able to replace all the communication aerials and would hopefully be able to re-connect with Earth very shortly.

It was now over 10 hours since the solar storm had ceased and yet there was still no communication from Earth or NASA or anyone else for that matter. Skylab XIII's safe orbit still placed it out of direct vision for communications so they would just have to wait.

As the Moon continued its normal traverse around the Earth, they were starting to get a better view of the

Earth, post the solar storm. What they could see from their high-resolution cameras was horrific. It appeared that every square inch of land looked white-hot and the whole planet glowed in the night sky. The view that Pat had come to love so much, that wondrous blue planet floating out in space, was now a glowing red and black colour.

They had also witnessed the tell-tale bright flashes of nuclear explosions which appeared more like multiple camera flashes at a major sporting event. Everyone who had remained in the hub was transfixed looking at the monitor as the flashes continued for almost two hours, and it was a relief when they finally stopped. If anyone had thought there was some hope of life left on Earth, the nuclear explosions destroyed all hope. Many staff who were no longer on active duty decided to go to their own quarters finding what was being displayed by the monitors as just too depressing to watch.

Both Pat and Frank came quickly to the realisation that Earth was not going to come to their rescue, they would have to go it alone! Pat gathered the senior team around them to begin the plan of how to survive on the Moon without the Earth. A concept they had hoped would never eventuate.

Pat led the initial discussion, 'We know that we can survive as we are mostly self-sufficient. Frank will take charge of all Earth rescue operations, as we must continue to hope that there will be survivors. There must be some people alive, especially those who were able to make it to deeper bunkers. It will be no use trying to save anyone from Earth; only to find that when and if we bring them here that they then die because we cannot support them!

Our priority is to ascertain if Skylab survived, as without Skylab any rescue mission is doomed before it even starts. Once we can re-establish communication with Skylab, they will need to be our eyes and ears.'

They discussed the finer details and then went to work.

It was sometime later that finally a shining dot appeared low around the edge of the Earth's atmosphere. Skylab XIII had survived after all! Frank tried the com-link immediately, 'Skylab, Skylab, this is Altai, do you copy, over?' 'Skylab, Skylab, this is Altai, do you copy, over?' He repeated over and over until he got a response.

'Altai, this is Skylab. Hi Frank, great to hear your voice and hope you Moonies escaped the worst. Skylab has come through the storm AOK. Apart from a few extra holes which we are trying to patch as best we can. Some of our electronics are still out, but nothing critical, over.'

'Skylab, that is fantastic news! And yes, we are all safe here and boy-o-boy were we happy to see you guys pop-up over the horizon! Neil, can you give us an update on things at home? We have seen that the solar storm has hit much harder than expected and you would have also seen multiple nuclear explosions which ringed the planet. Hopefully, some of your sensors can shed more information on what it is like down there, over.'

Neil then tried to give a detailed picture as possible, 'Thanks Frank, that's about right, what you have seen pretty well sums up what the sensors are showing us. Nothing could have survived on or even below the surface. We have not yet done a full rotation, so we have not seen everything yet, but the picture looks the same almost everywhere. During the height of the solar storm the temperature at the surface peaked in many areas well over 1700 degrees Celsius. All living creatures would have been instantly consumed and most structures and buildings would have melted and the resulting fires, well the result is obvious. Our initial readings from the atmosphere are that oxygen levels have fallen from 20 per cent to nearly non-existent at 0.002 per cent. Most fires have now run out of oxygen and temperatures are now falling. There is now little heat nor light being emitted by the Sun, as it appears to look like a large red glow in the sky, but we expect that as it is now a Neutron Star, its actual size is very small. As time goes on any heat is being quickly released into the atmosphere. There are currently no detectable levels of water vapour, which normally is around 1 per cent. But we anticipate that this may return relatively quickly. Any attempt to go to the surface will require oxygen and due to the nuclear explosions, radioactive protective suits will also be required. The length of any exposure will need to be limited as well. The extreme radioactive levels will remain in most parts of the planet over the next year, before beginning to fall to safer levels, perhaps in 30 to 50 years is our best guess.'

'With regard to potential survivors' Neil continued, 'we have only just begun scanning the planet on all available communication frequencies. It is early days yet and we will need to complete a few orbits before we can identify and communicate with anyone on the ground. We will keep you posted on this. Surprisingly, we have picked up nothing yet from NORAD, NASA, Crystal Peak or anyone official yet, which is not promising. We had expected at least some of them to be back online almost instantly after the storm had passed. We also fear that the nuclear strikes following the storm may have been more effective than what the experts predicted. We will keep trying, but the silence is not a good sign. And if they were knocked out, it gives us little hope for anyone else. There is just one piece of good news, we have been able to establish contact with a US submarine off the coast of China. They are in good shape and if there are survivors, they will be a key to any rescue attempts. That is the status as we know it Altai, over.'

While there really was not anything that they did not expect, both Frank and Pat just stared at each other, as hearing it out loud only made it worse.

Frank then soberly replied, 'Thanks for that report Neil. We on Altai concur with your understanding of the situation. Skylab's role is now critical to ascertain contact with anyone else on Earth, and we wish you luck. We will keep this channel open while you are in visual range. In about an hour you will be passing near the Earth Elevator and we are keen to know its status. From our end we will continue plans to either send you some extra people from here and pending contact with Earth, we may even have to bring you guys back to Altai. For now, you are our eyes and ears on Earth. Let us all pray that there may be some more good news soon, over.'

It was just over an hour later when Skylab delivered the best news yet. There appeared to be some areas that were not hit as severely by the solar storm. Thankfully, the Earth Elevator at Nauru appeared relatively undamaged at both ends of the snorkel. Although as they passed near the top of the Elevator, they could not detect activity from any of the robot workers. It was assumed that the pulse would have destroyed all their electronics. So, there was a glimmer of hope that there may also be other survivors.

Pat immediately sent for Jonsey to join them in his office.

'Jonsey, it looks like the Earth Elevator is still intact, we need you to re-activate our plans for Project Levitation and see if we can use the space elevator to both send people down to the surface and more importantly bring them back up. I will set up another team to work on the logistics on getting any survivors to the base of the Space Elevator. Frank can work out the logistics of how to get people from the Elevator back to Altai. Well, we all know what we must do, now let's get to it! We will reconvene daily at this time.'

chapter 30

BENDIGO (AUSTRALIA)

It was the dawn of a new day on a desolate planet. All the fires were extinguished due mainly to the lack of oxygen in the atmosphere. The sky had initially been totally clear however the first signs of clouds were slowly emerging. What Skylab could not detect was that sea levels were down, almost three metres across the planet – as much of the water had been consumed by the intense heat of the solar storm. Nearly the whole land surface of the Earth had been completely scorched. There was neither vegetation nor animal life. Forms of life that had survived for millions of years by burrowing into the ground were not spared this time as the heat was too intense. Most man-made structures had melted and now lay as piles of rubble.

Kaylan and the others had been transfixed by the radio announcements and slowly, one by one, the radio reports across Asia, Africa and Europe all went silent.

Kaylan had been sitting alone in a corner, like most lost in his own thoughts about what had happened above him on the surface.

Presently, the stranger who had escorted them into the mine walked across with his mother and introduced himself, 'Well young man, my name is Sam, Sam James and you are Kaylan, and I suppose you are wondering what this is all about?'

'Well, wouldn't you too if you found yourself deep underground, in a room full of strangers, where no one talks, but obviously are able to talk using telepathy or something, as I can hear you, but it is just noise!! And, just to add to the mix a solar storm may have wiped out the planet! I'd call it pretty strange, yes!'

'Yo slow down, slow down. Some things your mother and I will be able to make clearer for you, however why we are all down here, even I am not sure. All I know, like you, I felt the danger approaching and knew it was going to be bad for anyone still on the surface. We all had the same premonition to get as far underground that we could without knowing why. And now we are all here.'

'Yeah, but can you explain what you people are?' said Kaylan getting to his feet so that he was standing face-to-face with the man called Sam.

'All in good time, but first I have to tell you a story, one that will answer some of your questions. At the end of the story, you are going to have to make one of the most important choices of your life, one that we all have made. Now sit, calm down, as this will take some time.'

Sam then continued, 'You have already guessed that whilst we look like normal people, we are very different. It is because we are not from this planet. Just over two hundred years ago we discovered that our home planet Quanernia was going to be struck by a large meteor. Some of our best scientists were tasked with two major projects. The first team was to devise a system to divert the meteor away from our planet; and the other was tasked to work out a way to ensure the survival of our species. Unfortunately, the first group failed, and our planet was destroyed by the impact of the meteor. Billions were instantly killed and Quanernia was kicked out of orbit and the atmosphere destroyed. The second project involved assembling over 8,000 family groups into 2,000 escape capsules and sending them to 100 different planets where we hoped life may be able to exist. We have no idea whether the others have found safe planets; we only know what has happened here on Earth. Twenty capsules were sent to Earth, each containing a family of four. The capsules left our home planet at different times and different trajectories, arriving here over a 5-year period. The first capsule arrived on Earth in 1945, however, given the timing, we think that this capsule was the one that crashed into the path of Flight 19, a training group of five US Navy Avengers out of Fort Lauderdale over the Caribbean. The fighters and the capsule were destroyed with no survivors. Unfortunately for us, this accident created the mystery of the Bermuda Triangle and fuelled public interest in aliens and UFOs. The next four capsules came down safely in Australia between 1945 and 1946. The six and seventh capsules came down in New Mexico in 1947 and these became the most famous ones. Two more each landed in the USSR, South Africa and China, two landed safely in Florida and another two near San Francisco. Three never arrived. As you now know, the New Mexico ones caused us the most grief.'

'You don't mean Roswell, New Mexico?'

'Yes, I do and it became known as the Roswell Incident at the Foster Ranch⁹. Two of our capsules came down nearby, one at Socorro, about 240 kilometres west of the Foster Ranch and the other at Corona nearly a day later. From what we understand, trying to filter between the facts and the hysteria of the day, along with the deliberate cover-up by the US Government, we believe that the following sequence of events may have occurred.'

'At Socorro, the first capsule failed to land safely and crashed killing everyone on board. A group of archaeologists who happened to be in the vicinity stumbled upon the crash site of the alien craft and its occupants on the morning of July 3, only to be led away by military personnel. Further accounts suggest that the remains of this craft were shipped immediately to Edwards Air Force Base (known then as Muroc Army Airfield). The military then set up a fake crash site at the Foster Ranch using a combination of weather balloon debris and other materials to draw public attention away from the real crash site.'

'At Corona the second capsule landed safely in broad daylight. Unfortunately for them the area was crawling with extremely nervous military personnel, all armed. We can only surmise what happened, but we think that the military were so spooked by a potential alien invasion that they shot and killed some or all the occupants of the capsule. We know that a military mortician at Roswell Army Base undertook autopsies of those killed and treated one wounded alien from the Corona crash site. We think that the bodies were shipped from the Roswell base and then flown to Fort Worth and finally to Wright Field in Dayton, Ohio, the last known location of the bodies.'

'We had hoped that after the original reports the incident would simply go away and that we could then live quietly and in safety. Then again in 1995 the Roswell incident again came into public attention when a film purporting to show an alien autopsy was released. It began another flurry of activity with not only 'alien-chasers' looking over old evidence, but it also triggered the re-activation of the unofficial group of US counter insurgents which had been established just after the initial crash. This subsequent operation was nick-named *The Unholy Thirteen*[10]. They were tasked to hunt us down across the planet. And yes Kaylan, the authorities know of our existence. Luckily, so far, they have not found us! They know that more craft landed, but they just are not sure where or how many came or survived. In fact, they were almost correct, as there were only fourteen crafts which arrived safely, but the authorities do not know this for sure.'

'In 2002, a Sci-Fi Channel sponsored an excavation at the Socorro site in the hopes of uncovering any missed debris that the military may have failed to collect. Although their results turned out to be mostly unsuccessful, a University of New Mexico archaeological team did verify significant soil disruption at the exact location where witnesses to the landing reported seeing a long and linear impact groove. This allowed the Roswell story to continue and increased efforts against us.'

'It is only recently that we have been able to congregate and connect more easily with others here in Bendigo, San Francisco and South Africa. Of the original 80 sent to Earth, we are aware of only 29, but there could be more.'

'Kaylan, you do not realise just how special you really are. You are the first of our offspring to survive being born on Earth. Unfortunately, all our other children born here died either at birth or within the first six months. We are not sure why and obviously we have been unable to engage experts to undertake the research needed. But our guess is that it has taken this long for our own immune systems to begin to adapt to the viruses and bacteria found naturally on Earth. You are our future and give us all hope.'

'But you must be 100 years old or more?'

'In Earth year's yes, but in equivalent years we are about 40. Once we reach your age of around 18, we then age at about one in three Earth years. That means that you will live easily to the age of 200 Earth-years.'

'Wow! Said Kaylan.

'The downside has been that we have to relocate before people start noticing that we just don't age like they do.'

'So how can you speak to one another without talking? And why can't I?'

'Generally, we prefer to conduct what we call Hydran Ceremony around the age of what would be 25 Earth years. Until you complete this ceremony, our talking will just be an annoying noise, like static to you. Your mother still thinks you are too young to go through the ceremony, however the elders think that given the unknown circumstances on the surface, we had better do it sooner rather than later, and I totally agree. And as we are trapped here anyway, now is a good a time as ever. Well, what do you think?'

'What are the risks if I do the, what did you call it?'

'The Hydran Ceremony is rather difficult to explain. Put simply, it is a minor surgical procedure in the brain, the risks are low but you won't feel all that well for a couple of days after. I can only assure you that I have performed many of these, all safely, but it will dramatically change your understanding and life for ever!'

'It's so much to take in and I want to talk to my mother first.'

And Kaylan and his mother walked off to a group of three others that he did not know.

'Kaylan,' said his mother, 'I would like to introduce you to your father Dordain, and your two elder sisters Claire and Toyan. Both of your sisters were born on Quanernia. I am so sorry that I have kept this from you, however, we were very close to being caught several times. To increase our chances of survival, we split up in case one group was discovered, thereby protecting the whole group.'

Kaylan's mind was spinning with so much information. It was strange, even before his mother introduced them, he knew they were family and the feeling of love and warmth burned up within him. For the first time in his life, he knew where he belonged.

Kaylan was then introduced to all the other families. Sam James introduced him to his wife Jenny, and family members David and Graeme. Jim Bradley and his wife Mary and family members Jackson and Bowie and then to Chris Vernon and his wife Mandy and family members Jade and Nicole. They all talked for hours before they finally succumbed to sleep.

The morning brought a sense of new activity in the tunnel as a couple of the group had tried to reach the mine entrance but had to turn back due to the lack of air. Thankfully, their generator and air-scrubbers had so far been able to work continuously. On the next attempt to reach the mine entrance they carried oxygen with them as they disappeared up the dark shaft, with the wire from the emergency communication dish trailing behind them. After over four hours they returned exhausted and nearly out of oxygen. The lift was not working, as expected, and they had been able to climb to the top. Once near the top, they were able to see daylight through a very tiny hole but there was a huge amount of rubble, and what looked like melted steel blocking the top of the shaft. Using a long metal pipe, they were able to successfully push the pop-up antenna through the small opening and pushed it through as far as they could and just hoped that it was enough.

When they returned, they told everyone the bad news. Heavy excavation equipment would be required to get them out and it would have to be done from topside. Any attempt to try and clear it from below the blockage would risk it all coming down on top of them. They were going to have to wait for a rescue. The emergency antenna was going to be their only hope.

They connected the external antenna and to everyone's relief the emergency radio suddenly burst to life, 'this is Skylab, this is Skylab, broadcasting on all frequencies, please respond, please respond.......' They were saved!

'Skylab, Skylab, we are a group trapped down a mine in Bendigo, Australia, can you read us, over?'

'Bendigo, we read you 5 by 5, what is your status, over?'

'Skylab we are a group of 17 people. We are all safe

and secure but trapped deep down in an old gold mine. Our exact location is 36.7500 degrees South, 144.2667 degrees East, I repeat 36.7500 degrees South, 144.2667 degrees East. We are well provisioned with both food and water and if rationed it should be able to keep us going for around a month. We have sufficient batteries and fuel for our generators to maintain communications and air purifiers for a similar period. Can you please advise local authorities to come and rescue us, but they need to bring heavy equipment as the mine entrance is badly blocked by rubble, over?'

'Status noted. I am afraid to say that you will have to wait for rescue as there are no local rescue teams. I repeat, there are NO local rescue teams. Any attempted rescue will be many weeks away, if not longer, over.'

'We copy Skylab and will try and hold out for as long as we can. But can you tell us what has happened and how many other survivors you have found so far, over?'

'I will have to be quick as we are getting close to signal fade out. The solar storm has consumed most of the planet. Anyone that was on the surface or down to a depth of around twenty metres would have been instantly killed. The heat was so intense that it has burned and melted all structures. The accompanying pulses knocked out all electronic equipment and satellites. The storm consumed most of the oxygen on the planet and so those that survived, like you, have only survived by being deep underground with access to air via machines or through available air existing in the mine. If that was not bad enough, following the storm most of the world's nuclear arsenals either exploded on-site or automatically launched to their pre-determined targets. So currently radioactive levels in many areas are dangerously high. Your location seems to have avoided a direct nuclear hit, however every Australian capital appears to have been hit. To answer your other question, so far you are the only survivors that we have been able to communicate with. I strongly advise you to prepare for a much more prolonged period of being trapped in the mine and stretch your rations for as long as you can, over.'

'We had no idea that it was so bad. How do we keep communications with you Skylab, over?

'Our current orbit allows communication over Australia for up to a four-hour window. However, your signal is very weak, as we need to be nearly directly overhead to receive you clearly. Even now you are starting to breakup. I am now downloading information to you with the optimum communication times for the next month so that we can keep in touch and you can save on your battery power. At this stage we are coordinating rescue efforts with Moon Base Altai and we will do what we can. But you have given us hope that there will be other survivors. Our primary mission over the next few days is to ascertain what other groups have survived and to begin planning rescue operations. Better sign off for now until our next window, Skylab over and out.'

There was a collective sigh from everyone in the tunnel. Just when they felt they had been saved their closest rescuers were orbiting in space! It was impossible to believe that they may be the only survivors and that Skylab would not be able to do anything to save them.

As each day progressed the mood in the tunnel

improved every time Skylab came online. Even if the news itself did not improve. Just to know that there was someone out there really helped lift everyone's spirit.

It was about a week later that Sam walked up to Kaylan and asked, 'Are you ready to take the Hydran Ceremony? Let's go.'

Sam took Kaylan over to Chris Vernon and Jim Bradley who were already waiting for him and he was directed to lie down on a table where all three men stood around him. At first Kaylan was extremely nervous as they began to chant in a language he had never heard before. Eventually he found himself listening to the rhythmic tones of the chant and he began to find it soothing. He closed his eyes and he could hear Sam's voice above the chant, 'You are now in our hands, relax and just focus on my voice. You are about to enter the Hydran ceremony, a ceremony which has been conducted by our people for thousands of years. As you know you are the first of our children on Earth to reach the age for this ceremony. The ceremony consists of two parts. Firstly, we undertake a painless surgical procedure where we install a small connector between the two hemispheres of your brain. This will allow you to utilise the full potential of your brain as well as being able to communicate directly with all of us. The second part of the ceremony involves inducting you into our rich culture and history. This part you will find extremely tiring as your brain will absorb thousands of years of culture and history. At the end, you will fall asleep for at least 24 hours to allow your brain to absorb this new information. In addition, it allows your brain to repair itself as there is often swelling associated with the insertion of the connector. Once the swelling subsides you will wake up and feel like a vastly different person! Whilst you will still be the same Kaylan, you will have a whole new world to understand, one that is so completely different to what you have experienced on this planet. Now we will begin, are you willing to undergo this ceremony?'

'I do so willingly,' indicated Kaylan.

Sam picked up a long surgical probe and slowly inserted it into Kaylan's left ear. At the end of the probe a Nano connector was attached. After making a small incision to the ear drum, Sam placed the probe just in the right position and released the Nano connector. The Nano connector was programmed to move by itself through the blood vessels behind the ear drum and through the delicate brain matter to locate itself exactly between the hemispheres of the brain. Everyone had a slightly different brain composition, so the Nano connector was programmed to ascertain exactly where the neural networks could be optimised. Kaylan did not like the look of the probe and decided it was better to keep his eyes closed throughout the whole ceremony. After only a few minutes Sam announced, 'Great, the connector is now in position and is beginning to link into the neural networks of your brain.'

'How can you tell? asked Kaylan.

'You will be able to tell yourself in a moment.'

At first Kaylan felt nothing different. Then slowly he began to feel as if his whole body was becoming alive. He could not only hear his heart beating he could feel it, every contraction, he could even feel the blood rushing through his arteries. He found that he could control his whole body as well. All he had to do was to imagine his heart beating faster and it would. He found that he could traverse his whole body and sense the world from within every pore. Also, he found that he could recall events in his childhood as if they had just happened, remembering every vivid detail.

'I think that you are now ready to move to the second phase of the ceremony.'

With that announcement, all three men then moved in closer and placed their hands over Kaylan's head. At first Kaylan's head began to tingle and as he closed his eyes a pulsing bright light took over and drowned out all other thoughts. He tried to focus on one thought only but other thoughts crowded in over the top like a Tsunami. The pulsing light in his eyes flashed faster and faster until he could not tell if it was still pulsing. He then lost all sense of time and blacked-out.

Kaylan woke up not realising that he had been asleep for over 36 hours. He tried to sit up, but his head was still pounding so he decided to stay where he was. As he lay there, he found that the static in his head was now replaced by words, sentences, conversations and even pictures. Kaylan now knew what it was like to be a real Quanerian!

chapter 31

SKYLAB XIII

Skylab had now completed several orbits of the Earth post-storm and the grim picture had not changed at all in that time. After their initial success of contact with the USS Obama and the group of survivors in Australia, there had been only a few intermittent signals from other survivors.

They had been able to maintain regular contact with the group trapped underground at Bendigo and they appeared to be extremely well prepared and were not in any immediate danger.

They even had contact with a Chinese submarine off the coast of Japan. Despite the best efforts of the Skylab crew, the language barrier and the Chinese high sense of insecurity proved to be too difficult. The Chinese did not seem to be able to understand what had happened globally and became quite agitated and broke off all communications.

There was another group of survivors in Egypt. They were a group of French archaeologists who had taken refuge deep underground in the Valley of the Kings.

Despite warnings from Skylab about the dangers of going up to the surface, they were determined to try anyway. Since then, there had been no further contact.

Skylab also had a rather animated talk with an overly excited group of trapped miners in Chile. Unfortunately, from what could be understood they were already running out of water and supplies. Neil had explained the situation to them and when they fully realised that they were talking to Skylab and not someone locally, they must have realised that they had no hope of rescue. On the next orbit, they too were silent.

Skylab had also picked up a weak transmission from around the San Francisco Bay area, but it was too weak to be able to locate it exactly.

What surprised Neil the most was that it appeared that all the secure military bunkers had been taken out by a combination of solar storm, pulses or nuclear attack. They were all silent including the President's own bunker. Every now and then a new nuclear flash went off and it was impossible to say if they were targeted or had just detonated on their own.

Just as Skylab was passing over Japan, Neil saw another atomic flash.

He immediately thought of the USS Obama and tried to contact them, 'USS Obama, USS Obama, this is Skylab, do you copy over. USS Obama, USS Obama, this is Skylab, do you copy over.' He kept on repeating this message, but there was no response.

chapter 32

USS OBAMA (SOUTH CHINA SEA)

The USS Obama had been cruising at periscope level for some time hoping to pick up any signals from survivors. Buck turned to his sonar operator for an update.

Spike, his real name was Shaun Pike, but his name badge since day one in the navy was S. Pike, which was quickly shortened to just Spike. Spike was the sonar officer on the Obama, with a PhD in whale songs and was the first one to decode whale-songs into language.

Spike urgently announced, 'Commander, signal bearing 40 degrees, range 5,000 metres, ID it is a Chinese sub. Torpedo in the water, I repeat torpedo in the water.'

'Dive, dive, dive, ahead full power, let us get some distance,' yelled Buck.

'Torpedo 3,000 metres and closing.'

'Prepare counter measures, keep going deep.'

Buck glanced at the gauge and hoped they would be able to get deep enough in time. He noticed that all the crew were transfixed to their screens and keeping calm. They had trained for just this circumstance.

'Load torpedoes one to four, arm for micro-nuclear.'

'Torpedoes loaded, arming for micro-nuclear.' Came the response from the torpedo room.

'I authorise arming.' Said Buck turning the nuclear arming key.

'I co-authorise.' Responded the Executive Officer as he also turned his nuclear arming key.

'All torpedoes locked, loaded and ready.' Confirmed the torpedo room.

'Torpedo 1,000 metres and closing fast Commander.' Advised Spike.

'Release counter measures.'

The USS Obama had the latest in counter measures. Once released, small pocket drones produced holographic images of the submarine in a variety of locations. The drones simulated radar profiles and the usual noises that emanate from a submarine including water displacement.

There was no need for Spike to announce to the crew what happened, as the whole submarine was racked by the impact from the explosion produced by a torpedo.

'Spike, how close was that?' asked Buck

'The torpedo hit decoy number three Commander, fortunately for us it was the furthest away. Their torpedo was nuclear, a small tactical one. They mean business Commander!

'Where are they now Spike?'

'Heading bearing 345, range 5,600 metres, they are trying to hide behind the wake of the explosion.'

'Fire torpedos one and three.'

'Fire torpedos two and four. Let us see how they like these!'

Four torpedos, nuclear armed, sped towards the Chinese submarine.

On board the Chinese submarine the PR Tien, there was only confusion. Since the solar storm they had been completely isolated from Military Command. Their only order had been to dive, remain deep and prepare nuclear missiles for immediate launch. When they had tried to regain communications with HQ, the only response had been from Skylab and assumed that China had already been attacked. Unfortunately, none of the crew could speak English, a major oversight.

At first, they could not believe their luck, an American submarine was on the surface, like a sitting duck! Usually, US subs were so good at stealth. The captain ordered an immediate torpedo launch. There were cheers throughout the submarine when they felt the reverberations of the torpedo explosion. However, the sonar pings from closing enemy torpedos told them immediately that their initial torpedo had not been successful. Despite taking evasive manoeuvres, death was instantaneous as the PR Tien crumpled and was then vaporised by the small tactical nuclear warhead.

There were no survivors.

chapter 33

SKYLAB XIII

Neil had almost given up, fearing the worst for the USS Obama.

About an hour later he was relieved to hear, 'Skylab, Skylab, this is USS Obama, sorry for the delay. We ran into that Chinese submarine you told us about. Either they panicked or had standing orders and fired a nuke on us. Before they could fire another one, we had to take them out, over.'

'Thanks for that. We saw the flash and knew that you were in that vicinity. Glad to hear that you are safe, over.'

'Skylab, we have been unable to re-establish any form of communication with command, have you had any better luck than us? Over.'

'We have had no luck as well. We think that they must have all been taken out by the nukes. The people on Altai are developing a plan and they had better hurry. We will contact you again shortly, so stay on station, Skylab over and out.'

chapter 34

ALTAI (MOON)

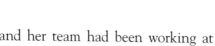

Pat and her team had been working at a frenetic pace and had not slept for days. Pat was just about to try and catch a catnap when she remembered the ultra-secure package that Dan had sent her along with all the other downloaded information.

It took an eternity to open the file, as she had to go through several different password and encryption levels. When the file finally opened, she was taken completely by surprise by what came on the screen.

'This information is only for the President of the United States or in an exceptional circumstance sent to the next authorised person where the President or the Government of the United States has been or has the potential to be disabled due to an extreme event. If the above event has occurred, you are now authorised by the President and the United States Government to use as you consider appropriate the following code. This code allows you to direct all US military, government, facilities and resources. Your one-time Authorisation Code is

Alpha EEE40547. With this code all such facilities that would normally be under the control of the President will respond to your orders or until rescinded by the President or representative of the Government of the United States with the over-ride code.'

'Please press continue if there is further briefing information contained in this secure package.'

Pat was in a state of shock and very cautiously clicked the continue button which continued blinking.

On her screen the next message read, 'This information is for the President's eyes only,' and there was a list of more than 50 top secret files. As Pat scanned the list she mused when she saw the title of file number 13, so the President's Book of Secrets was true!

Pat scanned quickly through the files and decided to click the file labelled *The Unholy Thirteen*, which had only been updated days prior to the solar storm. This file contained information about an alien invasion of the Earth which occurred between 1947 and 1951. The invasion appeared to involve up to 13 identified crash sites. It recounted details about one of the most famous crash sits near Roswell where one craft crashed, killing all four occupants. The second craft had landed safely but right next to a group of young, inexperienced and extremely nervous military personnel who thought the world was being invaded. They had immediately engaged in a firefight with the aliens and shot dead three and one died a few hours later in intensive care. It was noted on the file that the aliens appeared to have no offensive weapons. Before the fight began, the aliens self-destructed their craft so little was learnt of their technology, which was obviously far in advance of anything available on Earth.

The file contained extensive details and pictures of the autopsies which were carried out on all four bodies and it was determined that the aliens were externally very human-like with similar bone structures, but internally there were some unrecognisable organs.

Further reports and eyewitness account up to 1951 confirmed that at least another 11 crafts landed on Earth. In addition to Roswell, other sites were found in Australia, USSR, China, Florida and California.

Given subsequent investments in satellites and radar developments, the updated report indicated that there was no evidence to suggest that any other alien crafts have landed since.

'Interesting that they didn't connect the first craft in 1945 nor in South Africa.' Noted Pat who continued reading each report with interest.

As for the landing sites in the USSR and China, it was not surprisingly that no further information was available on file. It was assumed that all the crafts were of the same shape and size as that at Roswell, and each craft would have carried four aliens in a family-like grouping. Their reason for coming to Earth was stated as 'unknown,' but from what they gathered from the wreckage is that it was a one-way trip.

Despite the best efforts of the FBI and CIA, they had been unable to locate any aliens who may have survived, and it was assumed that they had either died or have successfully assimilated into the community.

There were no further actions recorded on file until

the late 1980's, when President Reagan requested that the file be reopened in preparation for a side meeting with key leaders as part of the Venice G7 meeting to be held in June 1988.

Pat continued reading.

The file contained a series of briefing notes from President Reagan. As she read through them it appeared that Reagan's interest arose from an earlier meeting with General Secretary Gorbachev in Kelsinki during May[11]. At this meeting, noted by Reagan, Gorbachev made a side comment to him at dinner about some aliens that they had captured soon after the American Roswell incident in 1947. He had joked with Regan as to whether the US had been fortunate enough to capture some of these aliens as well. From then on, Reagan had become obsessed for information about Roswell.

The next file note goes on to record the secret discussions which took place in Venice.

From Reagan's notes, he decided to inform G7 leaders, and a couple of other invited global leaders including China and Australia, about what had happened at Roswell and other landing sites in the US. He shared all the details of autopsies and the lack of any progress by the CIA and FBI since then.

Initially there was only silence and then Regan noted how glad he was when Gorbachev, whom he had given a heads-up before the meeting, informed the group about the Russian experience with these aliens.

From Reagan's notes it appeared that Gorbachev had dug deep into KBG records and eyewitness accounts. He outlined to G7 members that two alien crafts did land near the Vorkuta Gulag, a coalmining city approximately 1,900 kilometres from Moscow. Both crafts landed safely but were spotted by sentry outposts from a Prison Camp. All eight alien occupants had been quickly captured trying to shelter from the cold in an old farmhouse. Like Roswell, the aliens had been able to self-destruct their crafts so there was nothing that could be salvaged. The eight aliens were transferred secretly to Lubyanka Square in Moscow for interrogation and health checks. It was noted that the aliens possessed some form of telepathic power, as the Russians found that if you told one alien, even in total isolation from the others, they all knew!

Gorbachev indicated to the G7 that what happened next was loosely based on circumstantial evidence as all records had been destroyed, and everyone directly involved were executed under direct orders from Stalin. Gorbachev went on to describe that somehow the aliens were able to simultaneously kill all 200 prison officers and take control of the prison. The only way that the Russians could contain the 'situation' was to blow up the prison. Reagan noted that everyone was completely stunned.

In Regan's notes, Australia's Prime Minister Bob Hawke then outlined that they also believed that up to four alien craft had landed in Australia. Given remoteness and rugged terrain they had been unable to find any other traces, apart from evidence that crafts of some kind had crashed. Hawke agreed that a more concerted and coordinated effort must be made to track down these aliens.

Yang Shangkun, the President of the People's Republic of China also confirmed at the meeting that they also had two alien crafts which tried to land near Fusong in 1951. This was at the height of the Korean War and Fusong was close to the Chinese border with North Korea. The army at that stage of the war was expecting a US-led invasion and as a result, both crafts were immediately shot down and wreckage was strewn over a very wide area. They were assumed to be American planes and the incident was not even reported on official records. It was not until years later when local farmers found unusual wreckage and handed it in to the military that the incident was investigated further. Shangkun further indicated that so far, they had not had any success.

Reagan's handwritten note in the margin indicated that he was not fully convinced, if that is the interpretation of the handwritten words in the margin of the report, "bull shit!!!"

Reagan noted at the conclusion of the meeting that they would reconvene if further developments occurred because of increasing their efforts to catch any aliens.

There was nothing else recorded in the file after this meeting and with the end of Reagan's term of office it appeared that the whole issue became inactive.

However, Pat found a related file that had been created only a few years ago. A CIA Internal Report creatively linked mites, bees and Tinnitus clusters and found a correlation. The report appeared to be initially dismissed. However, because of the word 'mites,' this report had been referred to General Oliver, from Special Projects. He had then written a letter to the President noting the fact that the original alien autopsies had mentioned very briefly that the alien bodies appeared to have several small creatures over their body, possibly mites. These were never examined properly at the time and that DNA testing was not available. General Oliver sought permission to conduct another autopsy on the aliens, including DNA tests. The bodies of the four aliens had remained untouched since in storage at Area 49B.

General Oliver's autopsy report in the file proved that the mites which were killing bees, had the same DNA as the mites which were found on the aliens. His report went on to discuss how these mites have been spread by the surviving aliens. The report concluded by saying that these mites appeared to be immune to all current pesticides. However, the General also concluded that he did not believe that these mites had been deliberately released by the aliens as it appeared to be just part of their normal body make-up.

General Oliver's recommendations included tasking WHO, under the guise of a research project, to record and investigate all outbreaks of bee deaths and Tinnitus symptoms for any cluster to be secretly investigated by the CIA. His message was clear, "find dead bees, find Tinnitus symptoms and you will find aliens!" He also requested that a total media blackout on mites, bees and Tinnitus. He asked the President to give the Secret Service unlimited powers to hack computers, tail suspects, search and seize properties and to neutralise anyone who could be a threat. This was based on the potential widespread panic that would be caused by severe food shortages and confirmation that Earth not only had been visited by aliens, but that they were in the community. His report estimated, based on average human reproduction rates as a guide, that there could be at least 1000 aliens world-wide.

The President's approval was noted on the file.

Interestingly General Oliver's report also contained an attachment for the *President's Eyes Only* that provided an update on the success of the project that had been on-going for just over 100 years and had only recently resulted in scientists being able to re-create the material which had formed the outer lining of the alien space craft. This new material being extremely flexible and strong had led to improvements in the space program and had made it possible to construct the Earth Elevator snorkel.

'Ah ha,' said Pat, 'that's where the mysterious new material actually came from, I should have realised!'

The last file, which was only a few weeks old, was a CIA briefing report identifying specific alien nodes that were under active investigation. One grouping located in Bendigo, one in San Francisco and another in Johannesburg. The CIA expressed confidence that they were very close to apprehending all known aliens.

The final message appeared on the screen.

"Report End, please press continue to view other related reports."

Pat scanned quickly through some of the other files and then returned to the file on the *The Unholy Thirteen* and hit the delete button.

'Are you sure you wish to delete this file?'

'You bet!' said Pat, as she hit the delete button again.

'Hi Bos,' said Jonsey in his usual casual style as he walked straight into Pat's office. But he was taken aback by her grey and ashen face, 'You look like you've seen a ghost!'

'Just about, I'll tell you in a moment. Please call Frank

in will you and let's see how we are going to save these people.'

Once Frank arrived, Jonsey began his report on the plan to rescue survivors.

'Well, I think that we can adapt the Earth Elevator to get them off the surface by creating a vacuum in the snorkel. Using the same principle as that of using a hose and sucking water out at one end to get water to flow in reverse. We should be able to fit three maybe four people at a time, but they would all need to wear space suits with small air-boosters. My best guess at this stage is that it will take approximately 6 hours to make the one-way trip up the snorkel. It would be slow but could be made relatively safe for inexperienced people, if accompanied by one experienced officer. We then merely grab them when they pop out at the top of the snorkel, transfer them to Skylab and then they travel back to the moon in the shuttle. Simple!'

Both Pat and Frank loved the idea, 'But do we have enough space suits, boosters and fuel and how do we handle the transfers at either end of the snorkel safely?' asked Pat.

'Oh yes, we have plenty here for the job and we can package them up securely surrounded by one of our Helium-bags and shoot it down in the snorkel.' Pat then asked with a smile, 'What do you think Frank?

'Sounds fantastic to me. We can get the USS Obama to round-up as many survivors as they can fit on the submarine and take them to Nauru. They can manage the process easily at their end. We can ask Skylab XIII to re-task its orbit into a geosynchronous position above the Earth Elevator so that they can house the extracted survivors temporarily until we can transfer them to Altai using our usual sail process to drag the shuttle behind.'

'What about when they, as you say, 'pop' out the top?' asked Frank.

Jonsey had already anticipated this question, 'Well we merely catch them in a large net, like a spider's web, that they can bounce around safely in until we can catch them and take them to the airlock on Skylab. See, easy peesey!'

'Okay, we have a plan. Let us get Skylab and the USS Obama on the line.'

Once everyone was connected and relayed throughout Altai, Pat began the call, 'Welcome Skylab and USS Obama, this is Pat Milner on Altai. My authorisation code is *Alpha EEE40547*, I repeat authorisation code *Alpha EEE40547*, please acknowledge, over.'

Before this was acknowledged by the others, Frank and Jonsey just looked quizzically at Pat, as it was the first time she had mentioned or used any special authorisation code. They were going to be even more surprised by the response!

'Altai, this is Commander Buck Beckmann on the USS Obama, we also acknowledge your code Madame President and are awaiting your orders, over.'

'Altai this is Commander Neil Lavarche on Skylab XIII, as an internationally-based facility and in the absence of any other operating sovereign power, we acknowledge your code Madam President and await your orders, over.'

Frank, Jonsey and soon the whole of Altai immediately recognised the importance of what they had just heard. Pat was now the President of the United States and effectively of the whole Earth in the absence of any other sovereign power!

Pat then continued and outlined the key components of the plan as worked out with Frank and Jonsey only moments previously.

'Buck, I need you to prioritise which survivors to rescue first on the understanding that it is going to take us around 10 days to get our equipment and Snorkel crew on-site and prep the Snorkel for reverse flow. By then Skylab should be on-station near the Earth Elevator.

Any questions? Over.'

There were none, only nods from all participants on the monitors; they all had work to do.!

chapter 35

USS OBAMA (ON ROUTE TO SAN FRANCISCO BAY)

The Commander and crew of the USS Obama had the awful dilemma of deciding in which order they should try and rescue known survivors. The latest update from Skylab confirmed that there were three definite survival groups. The best prepared group of survivors so far seemed to be those in Bendigo, however they were located over 150 kilometres inland from Melbourne with no easy way to travel and retrieve them. There was a group in San Francisco where communications still had not been re-established and so they had no idea of the number nor condition of the survivors. Now there was a third group, a team of miners, while the actual number was unclear it appeared that they were also well provisioned but were trapped two kilometres underground in the Anglo Gold Ashanti mine in Kopanang, South Africa. This mine was also located inland, over 170 kilometres from Johannesburg.

Following discussions with other team members and the crew, Buck decided to head for San Francisco. San Fran had several benefits in addition to trying to save whoever was sending the signal. San Francisco provided an opportunity for the crew to say goodbye to home, and for some crew members it was home. The biggest plus for San Fran was that they should be able to access land transport and other essential resources that would assist them in their rescue efforts. This was because of the huge underground storage facilities at the Navy Supply Centre in Oakland. It was meant to be nuclear-bomb-proof after all!

After San Francisco they would head for South Africa via Cape Horn (as the Panama Canal would most likely be impassable. They would then head to Melbourne and finally to Nauru and the snorkel.

He ordered full power and they headed to San Francisco, three days sailing away.

Neil, on Skylab, had the job of informing the trapped group in Bendigo of the bad news; that they were still weeks away from being rescued and that they must try and stretch their supplies even further than originally intended. Surprisingly, they still seemed to be in good shape, considering their ordeal and thankfully they were well provisioned.

The signal emanating from San Francisco was still far too weak and they would have to wait for the Obama to get within range to make direct contact. South Africa had gone completely quiet and had not responded to any recent attempts to restore communications.

As the USS Obama sailed into San Francisco Bay Commander Beckmann relayed the periscope image throughout the sub, as well as Skylab and Altai. They all watched in horror as the USS Obama made its way around the twisted wreckage of the Golden Gate Bridge in the pale red light of day. All that was left of this majestic bridge was the melted stumps of the main pylons. They sailed carefully past the bridge to avoid the melted and twisted cables in the water. The last thing the Obama needed was to foul their propeller! Of San Francisco itself, which had been hit by the solar storm and then pounded by at least two Hydrogen bombs, there was nothing recognisable.

No one could have survived, thought Buck.

Once the USS Obama had entered the Bay, they had been able to locate the source of the weak signal to a sewerage treatment plant in Sausalito. They anchored as close as they could to the shore and immediately one Seal Team, in full safety gear, went to investigate the source of the signal and the other team headed for what was left of the navy stores in Oakland.

When the Seal team arrived at the sewerage plant it was completely unrecognisable from the surface. Using 3D GPS data files, they were able to locate an emergency stair-well. After considerable effort they were able to clear the rubble and access the stairs. They had a long walk down, as the control room, the source of the signal, was well over 25 stories below ground. Whilst a long climb down in heavy gear, the depth gave them some hope of finding survivors. Once they arrived at the base of the stairs, they forced open a fire door and edged along a darkened corridor. Their hopes began to rise when they could see a glow of light coming from under the door of the main control room of the sewerage plant.

When they entered the control room, they thought at first that the people there were just sleeping. But on closer examination it was clear that they were dead, all nine of them. It looked as if they all had died an agonising death. Severe radiation exposure can do awful things to people and the cause was easy to ascertain. The whole complex drew its air from the surface.

Unfortunately, it was never designed to be a nuclear fallout shelter.

The signal that was being sent was found to be an automated distress signal, which they subsequently deactivated and they shut down all systems.

The seal team then had to make the slow and painful climb back up the stairs to the top and returned to the Obama.

Meanwhile, the other seal team had more success. Accessing the file records of Navy ordinance, they were aware that the Navy had stores located in secret deep pens under the main dock yards. These storage pens were originally built during the Second World War but over time had been expanded and strengthened to withstand a direct nuclear attack. While they were easy to locate, just like the other seal team, it took a long time to remove rubble from the main access tunnels. Whilst the top levels were badly damaged and were inaccessible, the lowest level was accessible and completely undamaged.

Back at the Obama, Commander Beckman, like the rest of the crew had taken turns in getting topside. They still had to use safety gear and could only spend ten minutes maximum to look at the view, as the radiation levels were still extreme. From the port side, what was once Alcatraz was just a pile of unrecognisable rubble.

Suddenly there was ship-wide announcement, 'General quarters, general quarters, this is not a drill. We have unidentified in-coming. I repeat we have unidentified in-coming heading straight for us off the starboard beam – range one kilometre at 100 metres elevation and closing fast.'

The crew were quickly at their action-stations and ready for what-ever was about to come at them over the horizon. At first it was only a small spec on the horizon and then it appeared to split into six different objects.

'Let's take this slowly, hold your fire until we know what this is,' ordered Buck.

Through his viewer, Buck was then able to make out that they were six ultra-light helicopters heading towards them. And he knew that they could only be his seal team!

'Stand-down from general quarters, its our seal team returning,' he ordered. The noise from the ultralights now clearly heard as they gently landed on the main deck of the Obama.

Before leaving San Francisco, the seal team completed five trips to the navy yards and brought back spare parts, fuel, jack hammers and anything else they thought may be useful, before folding up the ultra-lights and stowing them away below deck.

Buck was pleased to be able to report back to Skylab and Altai that their mission was a success Even if they had been unable to bring back any survivors this time.

South Africa would take at least 10 days sailing at maximum speed.

chapter 36

BENDIGO (AUSTRALIA)

Kaylan and the group of survivors in Bendigo took the news about San Francisco badly. They had an affinity for any group of survivors, especially if they had been any of the other Quanernians. Now all hope rested on South Africa.

Daily life in the tunnel grew gradually worse. At the end of the sixth week, they had to turn off the small generator so that they could keep some fuel in reserve for communications only. They now lived in total darkness except when using their wind-up torches to move around the tunnel and prepare their meals. They had carefully rationed their food and water supplies, but the portions were now worse than meagre, and they were all feeling continually hungry.

No one had expected to be trapped for such a length of time and now they were in their eighth week. The stench from the tunnel was getting overpowering and again they were only able to run the air purifiers for a couple of hours each day. Their oxygen level was also continually falling, and they were becoming more desperate as time went on. Skylab had sent down some very useful details of how to make simple air purifiers which greatly helped to slow down the rate of carbon dioxide build up.

Kaylan used the time to try to catch up with his family and to better understand his culture and people. While information had been downloaded into his brain as part of the Hydran Ceremony, there was still a lot of content to interpret. He annoyed others with his endless questions, but for most of those in the tunnel, he was a welcome distraction from their dire situation.

At the beginning of the tenth week their radio gave out and no matter how they tried to repair it, it just would not work. They knew that rescue was still weeks away.

Now more than ever their tunnel felt like a tomb as each day passed.

chapter 37

EARTH ELEVATOR
(SPACE-SIDE)

Jonsey in the shuttle had a smooth and uneventful ride on the space sail and docked easily with Skylab XIII, which had already repositioned its orbit near the Earth Elevator. He received a very warm welcome from Commander Lavarche and his crew and they began immediately to prepare the Elevator. This was not going to be an easy task - to change the whole purpose, payload and direction of flow in the elevator. A team on Altai had constructed an exhaust and storage unit to attach onto the elevator and suck out and store all the air and thus create a vacuum within the elevator. This suction process had to be done every time they wanted to bring someone up as there was no decompression unit on the surface. The next task involved carefully packaging up 30 space suits and oxygen packs, along with several bulk oxygen bottles.

Jonsey installed them into the elevator for the trip down so that they would be waiting in Nauru at the base of the elevator when the USS Obama finally arrived.

Once the suction unit was attached and fully tested and functioning all Jonsey had to do was wait. So, like everyone else on Altai and Skylab, he kept a vigil near the communications section for any news. They had been informed of the outcomes from the rescue mission to San Francisco and were awaiting on the next stage of the rescue in South Africa.

Skylab now had no direct contact with either Kopanang or Bendigo.

Well, we are now ready for any survivors, if and when they come, thought Jonsey.

chapter 38

SOUTH AFRICA

The USS Obama arrived at Cape Town only to find the same level of devastation as in San Francisco. Once safely docked, a seal team headed off to the mine in the six ultra-light helicopters.

Everyone on board the Obama waited nervously in anticipation of what they may find, and it was not until later the next day when the first survivors arrived. They were all in an extremely poor condition and were immediately rushed into sick bay.

Over the next few days, the continuous shuttle of the ultra-lights continued until finally the last one returned and they immediately sealed the hatches and set sail for Australia.

As they began to dive, Commander Beckman made a sub-wide announcement, 'I am pleased to inform you that we have been able to rescue eight survivors from the mine,' a chorus of cheers broke out throughout the sub, 'however five are in a critical condition suffering radiation poisoning and severely dehydrated but they are in the capable hands of our Doc and his team. Three others are in a stable condition. Unfortunately, 31 miners had died before they could be rescued. We have now set course for Melbourne and I will update you when we have any news.'

At the end of the announcement, a member of the seal rescue team reported to their CO, 'Hey chief, you need to know something about those dead miners, well they were all indigenous, Khoisan people, I think! You need to investigate this; something it just not right!'

Their CO replied, 'Leave it to me, don't worry, I will look into it.'

chapter 39

BENDIGO (AUSTRALIA)

At first it was just a dull thud, followed by the sound of falling debris. Then is sounded and felt like an avalanche.

They were being rescued, finally after nearly 3 months!

It did not take long before bright beams of light bathed the tunnel. And then two big smiling Americans, wearing full protective gear walked in and one said, 'Hey did someone order a pizza?'

They took off their helmets and looked around the tunnel, 'I am Sergeant Brookes and this is Rating Officer Steven Jones from the USS Obama and, boy oh boy, if I were you, I'd get a new cleaner, this place stinks!'

At which everyone laughed as if they had never laughed before.

'Look, I know that you must have a thousand and one questions but please just hold onto them for now. We need to get you out of here ASAP! This is the plan, so listen-up! You will all need to move back down the tunnel and line up at the main shaft and we will help those of you that are unable to walk. We have oxygen, food and water for everyone. Once you are settled, we will then take you up the shaft one at a time as you will have to wear protective radiation suits and oxygen. Once on the surface we will transport you to the USS Obama which is docked in Melbourne. For the transport, well we have a treat for you, you will be travelling by ultralight helicopters which will take a couple of hours. Now this will take some time, so be patient, as some of you may be down here for some time yet.'

He saw the disappointed look on some of their faces and added, 'Sorry guys, you just have to be patient. In the meantime, please just relax and we will get you out of here as fast as we can.'

One of the rescued group members asked, 'Why so long? Surely….'

Brookes cut him off, 'We can only take one at a time up the shaft and we only have five ultra-light helicopters above and they can only carry one passenger at a time. In addition, we need to minimise the length of time you are exposed to radiation on the surface. And before you ask any more, when you get to the surface, you will be able to better understand the extent of the destruction and just how lucky you have really been!'

They all began the slow walk along the tunnel and collapsed with exhaustion at the end but very welcome for the oxygen, food and water!

The rescue processes up the shaft began with Kaylan, being the youngest. At the base of the shaft, he was provided with a radiation suit, oxygen and helmet. He was placed in a harness and then once the signal was given by Brookes, he began the slow ascent up the shaft to the surface.

At the surface he was grabbed by another US Marine and was shuffled towards one of the five ultra-light helicopters. Once he was clipped-in the pilot took off. Kaylan looked around but there was nothing except a barren and black landscape. Every now and then a shard of metal protruded into the air to delineate what might have been a building or bridge. Looking up at the sky, the Sun was only a red glow, and even in the protective suit, he could sense the colder air. During the flight to Melbourne all he could see was the same desolate scene, with the only exception being that as they approached the central business district, the pile of rubble was considerably higher. Then he saw the submarine moored at a dock at the top of Port Phillip Bay. They carefully landed on the deck of the sub and Kaylan was quickly ushered below.

The ultra-light was quickly refuelled and took off again heading back to Bendigo. This process was repeated over and over until all survivors were safely on board.

The news of the safe arrival of all 17 survivors on board the USS Obama was excitedly received by both Skylab and Altai.

Commander Beckmann ordered the hatch to be sealed and they sailed out of Port Phillip Heads for Nauru.

chapter 40

USS OBAMA
(EN ROUTE TO NAURU)

It took a few days to conduct detailed health assessments and for all the new survivors to settle into life on an operational submarine. Once these checks were completed for all survivors from Bendigo, they were then invited to meet in the USS Obama briefing room.

The room was ridiculously small and noisy when Commander Beckmann stood in the doorway, as he could not even squeeze into the room itself, 'Ah hum, if I could have your attention, please,' and paused until the chatter subsided, 'for those that I have not met, I am Commander Beckmann, and I would like to warmly welcome everyone on behalf of the crew of the USS Obama. It is our great pleasure to see any survivors from this horrendous holocaust. As you may have been informed, we also have eight other survivors from a mine in South Africa in sick bay, who are still too weak to join us. I know that you have many questions and until now we really have not had the time to answer them. Today I want to tell you what we know and then outline the next stage of your journey. Firstly, I congratulate you for your planning and sacrifice over the past few months, you could not have found a better nor more provisioned place to take safety. Without it, and your efforts, you would not have survived. Unfortunately, many others who also sought shelter in mines, basements and underground car parks were not so lucky. The solar storm and related pulses have destroyed all life on Earth as we know it. The heat generated by the solar storm melted metal and most building materials. I am sure you all witnessed this destruction as you flew over what was left of Melbourne. The pulses knocked out all electronic equipment including satellites. The cause of the solar storm we do not know nor understand. To add to the problem, either due to the extreme heat or the pulses themselves, nuclear missiles were launched across the globe. For the few people that survived the solar storm, they did not survive the nuclear blasts and the resultant extremely high levels of radiation. Skylab recorded over 2,000 nuclear detonations across the planet. Well, that is enough of the bad news, now for some good news. Skylab and Altai Base on the moon, came through basically unscathed by the solar storm and pulses. These were both saved more by good luck, due to their relative positions and orbits at the time when the solar storm struck. Since the storm, Skylab has been scanning on all frequencies for any signs of life and quickly they identified signals from groups in Chile, Russia, Egypt and Florida. Unfortunately, they all fell silent within the first couple of weeks.'

After a short pause Beck continued, 'fortunately parts of the Pacific were not as badly exposed to the solar storm nor suffered direct nuclear blasts, including the Earth Elevator on the island of Nauru. I will say more about the importance of this facility in due course. Skylab will continue to look and scan for life, but we are not hopeful. Now I will open up for your questions.'

There were a range of questions and the Commander thoughtfully responded to each one.

Looking around the crowded room the Commander then said, 'Are there any more questions? Well, if there are no further questions about what happened, I would like to give you a sense of what is going to happen next. The Altai team has developed a plan to resettle you all to the Moon,' and he paused for everyone to take in the significance of what he had just said.

'We are now heading at full speed for Nauru and the Earth Elevator. As some of you may know, the Earth Elevator was constructed to ship Helium-3 and other mined material from the Moon and take it from the edge of the Earth's atmosphere down to the ground by gravity. This material was then loaded at Nauru onto ships and sent world-wide for processing into fuel for power plants. When we arrive at Nauru, you will enter the Earth Elevator in small groups and fitted into full space suits, which have air boosters attached to allow you to move up to the top of the Earth Elevator. Each group will be escorted by an experienced astronaut from Altai. Once you reach the top you will be transferred to Skylab XIII, which has now been moved in orbit close to the Earth Elevator. From Skylab you will then take a much more luxurious flight on the shuttle to Altai, your new home. Now are there any questions please?'

'Why can't we just live on Nauru?

'Actually, there are a couple of reasons. Firstly, the level of radiation will eventually kill you. Most of you have already exceeded safe levels of exposure, even the radiation levels at Nauru are far too high. We expect it will take at least 3-5 years to come down to anything close to safe levels. In addition, as you already know, oxygen levels in the atmosphere are almost non-existent and we have no idea how long it is going to take for a breathable atmosphere to be re-established, perhaps never.'

'Commander, you said we have exceeded safe radiation levels already, will we get sick, or even die as a result?'

'None of you have so far shown any signs of permanent damage, and the checks that our Doc has now completed indicate that you all should be fine, with no long-term radiation effects.'

'Can we all fit on Altai?

'Yes, you all can. Currently there are around 200 who call Altai home, and its capacity is closer to 300. So, there is ample space and sustainable water and food available. Next week, there will be a briefing by the Altai team to give you better understanding of how Altai works, what it is like to live there and answer any questions or concerns that you may have about living on the Moon.'

'Will you and your crew be relocating to Altai as well?'

'In the longer-term this is the most likely scenario. Firstly, we will continue to search for any other survivors. And secondly, Altai is developing an extensive shopping list of equipment, stores and other items that just are not available on the Moon. We know there are bunkers that house such supplies scattered across the globe that should be intact.'

With no further questions, the briefing session wound-up, and the Commander and his crew went on with their assigned duties.

Most of the survivors stayed seated and quietly discussed the implications of relocating to the Moon.

For the Quanerian survivors, they had survived the death of their own planet, and so they all knew they could do it again. In many ways it was going to be a lot simpler this time!

The journey to Nauru was uneventful. The 17 Australian survivors crammed into the forward torpedo compartment and the eight South Africans were housed in sick bay. They all spent their time comparing stories and generally trying to keep out of the way of the crew as they went on with their routine tasks. Their meals and bathroom times were sequenced so as not to interfere with the operations of the crew and to give them all some elbow room in the cramped conditions.

chapter 41

NAURU

When they finally reached Nauru, Beck was pleased to see that the main wharf was in relatively good condition, unlike the rest of the island which was barren scorched earth and rock. A seal team undertook a flight around the island, but as expected they found no survivors.

Another seal team had the job of undertaking repairs to the Earth Elevator and to retrofit it to allow the transfer of people rather than just receiving cargo.

It only took a couple of days to complete this job and then they were ready to begin to transfer the first survivors up the snorkel.

The process involved entering the airlock at the base of the snorkel where there was only room for four people. Each person was then fitted into a space suit and their escort astronaut carefully checked their suits and individually went through the safety procedures, the features of the suit, the controls and the numerous heads-up display screens which monitored everything. They then tested their air boosters and conducted a final check. After everything was double-checked again, the process for removing the air in the snorkel began. When zero pressure was achieved in the snorkel, the airlock was also cleared and a green light indicated it was safe to enter the snorkel. Once inside the snorkel it was then possible to use the air boosters to ascend. This part of the journey took up to 8 hours and three oxygen tanks each. At the top of the snorkel, they flew uncontrollably out into space, only to be caught by a strategically placed net, along with six other astronauts who acted as 'catchers.' Once caught they were then taken to Skylab.

The first group of three were transferred without any issues, and then they transferred the injured South African survivors, which took a lot longer as they went up one at a time and were supported by two astronauts. Kaylan and his family had to wait for over two weeks before it was their turn.

It was not long before all survivors were then transferred from Skylab safely to Altai on the shuttle.

The Obama then secured the Earth Elevator for when it became their turn and set sail to try and fulfill Altai's huge shopping list.

chapter 42

ALTAI (MOON)

Both Pat and Frank, whilst initially disappointed by the extremely low number of survivors, were also quietly pleased, as it made it so much easier for them to handle, given their limited room and resources. All survivors went through a detailed induction program for Altai and were assigned to their quarters. The next formal step would be to allocate them to tasks and train them accordingly. Most of them would begin working in the unskilled areas such as the greenhouses or in the kitchens. After a while they would then be reassessed based on each person's skills and determine how best they could be used to benefit Altai. At this stage it was felt more important to quickly give them roles and keep them busy.

They would also need more time to work out how to eventually transfer the crews of the USS Obama and Skylab to Altai as they could not remain where they were indefinitely. There were 150 personnel on the USS Obama and another three on Skylab. These numbers would place great pressure on the current space available and resources.

Fortunately, both assets still had key roles to perform, so long as they didn't break down!

Frank and his team had prepared an enormous shopping list for supplies and equipment that they needed now and into the future. Whatever the crew of the Obama could find from this list would be extremely helpful. The most difficult part in developing this list was limiting it to items that were either small or could be dismantled into small pieces to fit within in the narrow snorkel. It was never designed to play such a role and yet it had worked perfectly in bringing survivors off the surface.

At the end of the first week after most of the survivors had settled in, Pat led a Memorial Service. The service was simultaneously beamed to the crews of the USS Obama and Skylab. Skylab also relayed it through all known frequencies on Earth. They did not know whether there was anyone left alive on the surface, but there just may be someone who could hear their message but not transmit. And anyway, they all thought it was the right thing to do.

Once everyone was assembled in the Altai cafeteria, Pat began.

'We are all gathered to remember those that we have lost. No one was prepared for such an awful disaster and yet once again we have all been reminded of just how small we are in the scheme of the Universe. We have lost our home and now we must make a new world, one vastly different from where we were born. For those who had already made space their home, you will have to adapt to a new way of doing things and be inclusive to our new family members. The safety-net of the Earth is no longer there to provide us with comfort. For our new family members, we understand the difficult transition that you will have to make over the ensuing months. You will need to take on duties that you have never done before, essential for our survival. Altai was never designed to be totally self-sufficient from Earth, so we will all have to be creative if we are to survive. We know that the Earth that we all love is no longer. Nor can we ever expect to return or become complacent in thinking that we can return. I know that I can trust and count on your support as we face the new dawn. Considering our new future together, the senior team have decided to rename Altai, to Earth2. One to keep the legacy of where we have all come from and secondly to announce that we all now begin a journey towards an uncertain future. God bless us all.'

There was nothing to celebrate and the solemnity of the occasion overpowered everyone. They all had a lot of work to do if they were going to survive.

It was a couple of weeks after the memorial service when Pat was in her office developing new plans for the possible expansion of Earth2 when the Base Doctor buzzed to say that he needed to speak to her urgently.

'Thank you, Madam President, for seeing me, I have wanted to see you for some time but not until I had completed my assessments for all of the survivors.'

'Is there a problem?' Pat enquired.

'At first, I thought what I was seeing was trivial. I have patients present to me with what are symptoms of Tinnitus. This condition consists of noises in people's head like a ringing or static noise. From what I could gather, none had any previous symptoms or such a complaint before. At first, I put it all down to delayed trauma and prescribed some tablets and hoped it would all go away. But it has not, and in fact it seems to have become worse! I have now checked all the records and we seem to have two very distinct patient groups. One group, comprising only of Moonies, experiencing the ringing sound in their ears. Whilst annoying, it is not life threatening. The second group is of more concern, our survivors, except for a couple of the more injured South African survivors. When I first examined them upon their rescue I was totally amazed by their physical condition, given their experiences. They just do not seem to have any health issues, not even a common cold or a headache. Since they came here, they have not required any medicines and they never seem to have any complaints. Not one of them has needed to come into the clinic. And yet most Moonies are in once a week, if not more. This survivor group are just something else!'

'What are you trying to tell me Doc, you're not happy because some people don't need your services?'

'Well yes, and no. I really don't know what to make of it. The survivor group are just not normal people!'

'What do you want me to do about it?'

'Nothing, no nothing. Perhaps I am looking at this the wrong way around, but I just had to tell someone.'

'Look doc, you go and run some more tests. Use the excuse of residual radiation tests or whatever. Take a couple of weeks and come back to me with your results. For now, we will just keep this under your hat, okay?'

The doctor left Pat's office feeling slightly better. However, the more he thought about it the more he felt there was really something different about the group of survivors. He had some more tests up his sleeve and this time he would use his DNA screening tests as well. He had been hoping to save these types of tests for some future use, as he did not have any way to replace or create the DNA testing equipment. But he just had to know what made this group different!'

Once the Doctor left, Pat immediately called Frank into her office.

'I'm afraid the time has come.'

No one seemed to question the death of the base doctor from a sudden heart attack. It was assumed that like everyone he had been under extreme stress and his heart must have just 'given out.' Conveniently for Earth2, one of the injured survivors from South Africa, Dr Basson, was a medical doctor and now that he had fully recovered, he could take over this most important role.

chapter 43

USS OBAMA & SKYLAB XIII

It would be another four months before the USS Obama completed its mission. As anticipated, no other survivors were found, however the scavenger hunt had proved extraordinarily successful and it provided some particularly useful equipment and spares for Earth2.

In the end, it was Commander Lavarche who finally pulled the pin on the Obama's mission as life in space was becoming more dangerous as time went on. Previously Skylab tracked the orbits of the thousands of pieces of space junk, but since the storm these records meant nothing as there was now a whole lot more debris whizzing around the Earth. Skylab's normal orbit was too high for most of this junk, but in moving to the lower orbit to take up a position near the top of the Earth Elevator, it now brought a much higher risk. It was only a matter of time before Skylab and the Earth Elevator both would soon be shredded to bits by space junk coming their way. Time was running out, they all had to leave!

It was not long into their final return voyage to Nauru

when the worst thing that could happen to a submarine occurred. An explosion in the torpedo room. At first, the crew thought that they were all going to die as the sub sank perilously close to its crush depth. Fortunately, the automatic air-lock doors held and the sub was finally able to right itself and slowly limp back up to the surface on emergency power.

They were able to slowly sail back to Nauru with a large hole on the starboard side. However, twenty-three of the crew did not make this final journey, including the ship's doctor.

But fortunately, their job had been completed and they commenced the final transfer to the Earth Elevator and to their new home, Earth2.

With Skylab refuelled and restocked it made a much slower journey, not to a new orbit around Earth, but into a new, stable and much safer orbit around the moon.

chapter 44

EARTH2

There was a major celebration when the crews from the USS Obama and Skylab were all transferred to Earth2.

Earth2 was no longer a mining base, it was now a fledgling colony. At first their only aim was to ensure survival and achieve a new level of self-sufficiency. Now with a broader range of experts on-site, along with everything the USS Obama has scavenged from storage depots across the planet, there were new possibilities. Both Pat and her small team of geologists began searching for more useful resources that they could extract from the moon.

Kaylan and all the Quanernians had settled well into their new home. They also felt very safe on Earth2 and whilst they could telepathically communicate right across Earth2, they kept this to a minimum as now they knew that some people were affected.

Kaylan also felt so much better now that they had been joined by other Quanernians. He was still in awe of their history and how well they had planned for the survival of their species, not only from Quanernia, but also on Earth.

As Kaylan sat watching the celebrations wind-down, he thought to himself, which was also received instantly by every other Quanernian on Earth2, 'It really couldn't have worked out better if we had caused the solar storm ourselves!'

From the other side of the room, Dr Basson was also watching as people started to leave and return to their quarters and heard Kaylan's comment, but isolating his own comment to himself, 'Little do you know, young fella!'

chapter 45

EARTH2-BUNKER
(ONE YEAR LATER)

Harvey Claire was out of breath as she was running late for a most important meeting! As she struggled to climb through a tangle of cables, water pipes and ventilation ducts, her mini-oxygen pack became snagged on a pipe riser clamp and nearly took her head off. She wasted what seemed like an eternity to free herself and reach down for her oxygen mask which had become wedged. Once free, she continued making her way through the shaft, muttering to herself, 'Why am I doing this? Why am I doing this?'

Harvey, Earth2's Food Production Manager, enjoyed being one of the original Moonies. She was born and spent all her childhood in Christchurch, New Zealand and then had moved to Toronto, Canada to live with Jerome, her husband. They had met under difficult circumstances, under about 20,000 tonnes! Harvey had driven into work like any other day into the CBD of Christchurch. She had just parked her truck in the lower-level car park at work and thought at first that she must have accidently hit a pole when the whole building seemed to shake and then everything seemed to cave in before her eyes. The very next thing she remembered was seeing a smiling man's face upside down in front of her saying, 'Bonjour' and then she felt the pain.

When she woke up next, she was in a hospital bed and there was the same smiling man as before. At least he was not upside down this time!

It took weeks before she was well enough to be told what had happened. Christchurch, which had been almost destroyed by earthquakes in the early 2000's was again hit by a massive 8.7 Richter scale quake which totally devastated the city this time. Her building, despite being designed to be quake proof, had proven inadequate to cope with such a massive quake and it had completely collapsed. Harvey was informed that she was the only one pulled out alive, just over five days after the quake. She had been saved by a combination of factors; her truck was an old solid land cruiser and the pillar that she had parked next to had held and provided some added protection. Her right leg was severely injured and was close to being amputated on-site, but thanks to her smiling angel, it was not. And while she still walks with a slight limp, she would not be alive if not for this man's persistence with other rescuers and doctors. The smiling man, who came to see her every day during her recovery and rehabilitation, was called Jerome. He was part of an international rescue team sent into Christchurch to search for survivors and help identify the dead, of which there were so many!

Jerome became a huge part of her life and they married

Nova

while she was still on crutches, just four months after being pulled from the rubble. As soon as she was well enough to travel, they moved to the French Quarter of Toronto and had two children, Sonia and Christine. Harvey's life was content until just before their fifteenth wedding anniversary when Jerome was diagnosed with an aggressive form of brain cancer and died three weeks later.

Harvey went through the motions of the funeral and in the weeks and then months afterwards, found herself longing to return home. So, she packed everything up and was just about ready to return to New Zealand, when she noticed an advertisement seeking experts in food management with a preference for family groupings. However, it was for a one-way journey to the proposed Altai Moon Base. At any other time, Harvey would not have even considered it, however as she was already packed and her two children ready to move, she thought, why not!

No one was more surprised as Harvey when after a gruelling series of meetings, interviews and tests, they were all accepted. After a further twelve months of intensive training her family were transferred to Altai Base on the Moon to join the other Moonies.

Altai at that stage wasn't much to look at. It consisted of a series of empty chambers cut into the Moon rock and accommodation was rough. Fortunately, Sonia and Christine didn't seem to mind and there were so many other teenagers growing up in such a unique environment - to them, it seemed just like a long school excursion!

Harvey oversaw all food management, which involved growing food in the large greenhouses, livestock management, genetic food production and along with managing kitchen and cafeteria, including all staff. Her role was an essential operation given their location.

Harvey could not believe that her family had now lived on the Moon for nearly ten years and her two children were now young adults. Sonia was following in her footsteps in Food Management and would soon take over Harvey's role. In fact, she was experienced enough now to do so! Christine also worked in the kitchens and was turning into a particularly good chef. Whilst they both would flirt with some of the miners, neither daughter seemed interested in anything steady at this stage. Perhaps it was just that the options were so few! Like everyone else, when the crew of the USS Obama came to Altai, she thought that her girls, and most other 'un-hitched' Moonies on the base, would most likely hitch up with one of the crew, but they had proved to be a very close-knit group.

As the colony needed to grow, it would not be long before the question of mating with someone would be forced upon them if they did not act!

As Harvey continued to make her way through the tangle of pipes and wires to the Bunker, she realised just how important this meeting was. In the first 12 months since the creation on Earth2, so many Moonies had died. It had been explained to them by the new Doctor Basson, as the Moonies had been isolated from viruses on Earth, their immune systems just could not cope. Whilst most of the new arrivals were immune to these, the Moonies were not. Of the original 200 Moonies, only half had survived, so the population of Earth2 was now around the same number as at the beginning of the crisis. This had in some ways made Harvey's job easier, as she believed that food production would not have been sufficient to support the numbers once the Obama crew joined Earth2. Harvey felt that her family had been blessed and saved from death. Perhaps it was because they were more used to handling food and therefore practised better hygiene than others, or they were just bred healthier coming from good New Zealand stock!

She was just thinking about some of the other changes over the past year, some good, some bad, when she finally saw the light from the Bunker vent.

Upon entering the room through the access vent, she found that they were all present and that she was the last one to arrive, again!

'About time Harvey, we were beginning to worry about you. You know how dangerous our meetings are becoming!' said an extremely nervous Nancy.

'I'm sorry I'm late, but that Dordain, he is just a nasty piece of work. He was at the glasshouse again inspecting the camera systems and interrogating my staff over last month's incident.'

'Yes, he's been everywhere recently, they are up to something that's for sure. How much do you think they know already?' added Jim.

'OK, OK, we need to get started shall we, as we can't be all seen to be gone for too long? said Harvey, who had taken the 'un-elected' role of convenor of this secret group.

'Orley, before we start, I have a very important new member to welcome to the meeting.'

Everyone looked at each with a high degree of scepticism, as they were now a very tight and select group after nine months of regular meetings. Harvey could see the concern in everyone's eyes, as it had taken a long time for them to become comfortable, given the high risks, and continued, 'I would like to welcome Commander Buck.'

Commander Buck emerged from the same vent that Harvey had entered from.

"As we all thought, continued Harvey, 'we assumed that you, Commander, may have been one of them. But I now know we were wrong, thanks to Spike doing some checking and by the behaviour that the *Others* have shown to you. We know now that you are not one of their inner circle.'

'Well, I am glad to hear that,' replied Buck. 'I knew immediately that something strange was going on here, but just could not put my finger on it. That is why I have tried to quarantine the crew and keep them operationally separate the whole time until I could figure the lay of the land, so to speak. It was Shaun here, who finally filled in the missing pieces and introduced me to Harvey. I am here to help in every way that I can, not to take over.'

Shaun, then added, 'Thanks Commander, I was a good friend of Dr Ben Jones, the USS Obama doctor, and he had shared with me his suspicions about the rescued people and how different they seemed. When he was killed in the torpedo room explosion, I started looking more carefully at all the survivors who came onboard and began the watch-list that we have all been working on since. We know that they must possess some form of telepathic power and seem to be able to easily communicate together across the whole base.'

'How many *Others* are there? asked Buck.

'Every rescued Australian is on the list, that makes

17. I have now also confirmed that every rescued South African, including Dr Basson, should be placed on the list, making a total of 25.'

'What made you finally add them to the list? asked Harvey.

'I finally was able to chat to one of the marines who rescued them. As we all know the marines are a tight-lipped group. He was very concerned about the deaths of the indigenous miners and suspected that they may have been murdered. He reported the matter to his CO at the time, who said he'd investigate it. But nothing ever happened.'

'Keep going Spike, tell them what else you told me,' said Buck.

'Well, this placed the marine's CO, Captain Gunn squarely on my watch list. He had not reported the incident to Commander Buck as he was required to do so at the time. It was when I told Buck, sorry Commander Buck, that he told me he already had concerns about Captain Gunn as being a possible saboteur, setting the explosive that killed 23 crew members including the ship's doc on our final journey back to Nauru. He was the number one suspect, but there was no evidence.'

'I don't think the USS Obama was ever meant to have made it back at all,' said a solemn Buck.

'So, we have 26 on the list, including Captain Gunn.' Spike continued, 'Then we have Commander Lavarche and his two other crew members and even now, I still find it hard to believe but also our Madame President, second in charge, Frank and our two Chief Miners Jonsey and Otis, making a total of 33.'

The room was totally silent digesting the enormity of their task, until Harvey broke the silence, 'It is really unbelievable that any Moonies could be, aliens? We have worked so closely with some of them for so long, and I had no inkling, at all. And to think that my Sonia likes Kaylan, and I have been pushing them into thinking about getting married someday! Okay, let's move onto what we are going to do, before we are all missed, so over to you, Orley.'

'Thanks Harvey, and er ar welcome Commander. Well, it is now confirmed that there will be a one-year anniversary event in two weeks. Fortunately, I have been put in charge for all the arrangements. However, as far as the *Others* are concerned, I don't think that they are all that much interested in the one-year celebration, as they seem to have a higher sense of excitement, as if something major will be finished at about the same time.'

'That's interesting,' said Spike, 'as there has been a lot of activity to and from Skylab. They seem to building something on Skylab that they don't want anyone else to know about. But just what they are doing, I am not sure.'

'Do you have any ideas Spike?' prompted Buck.

'Well, I still need to do some more checking, however I think it could be a new communication satellite dish.'

'Who do you think they could be wanting to talk ...' Harvey didn't even have to finish the sentence, as they all realised.

'Is there any way that we could slow their work down or destroy it, Spike?' enquired Buck.

'The problem is that the *Others* are in total control

of Skylab and the shuttle flights. We just don't have a chance, without them knowing and stopping us.'

Virtually simultaneously, Harvey and Buck said, 'We will just have to find a way to stop them before it is active!'

And everyone nodded in approval.

'We'd all better get back to our posts. Spike, Orley and Buck, we need to meet tomorrow and work out a plan.'

Harvey closed the meeting, they all then climbed back through the ventilation shaft and used different exits to not cause any suspicion.

chapter 46

SECURITY CENTRE
(PENTHOUSE)

While the secret meeting in the Bunker was taking place, a similar special meeting was occurring in Security, where President Pat was receiving an update from Dordain, her Head of Security, at the Senior Executive Team Meeting.

'We are still a few weeks away from completing the satellite dish, so it looks like we may not be ready for the one-year celebrations.'

'I thought we were almost good to go,' said Frank frustratingly.

'Yes, so did I, but it is what it is.'

'And how are you going penetrating Commander Buck and his crew. They still are basically segregated from everyone else?'

'Well,' responded Dordain, 'they are proving exceedingly difficult. Unfortunately, the failed attempt to sink the Obama has made him very suspicious and there are just too many of them now to handle in the usual way. We will have to come up with another solution.'

'You had better solve it soon, or I will get someone else to do your job,' Pat said more angrily then even she expected.

Whilst no one else in the room neither sensed nor saw, Dr Basson gave a wry smile.

Dr Basson had held a senior position in Emperor Quaylan's Office on Quanernia and still saw himself as the future leader. No one could have predicted how hard it was going to be when their crafts had landed just outside Cape Town. The South African Government controlled everything, movement was difficult and security was intense. Without IDs, the only opportunity that his group had was to initially work in the gold mines and work their way up the pecking order. Over time they were able to build IDs and cover stories. Also, by being so physically isolated, Dr Basson and his group had no way to easily contact or find other Quanernians.

Whilst Dr Harris remained on duty with the USS Obama, and the sudden death of the colony doctor, conveniently Dr Basson was the only person able to take on the role of colony doctor. And whilst it had been unfortunate that the USS Obama had not been sunk in the torpedo room explosion, luckily Dr Harris had been killed, ensuring that Dr Basson could operate more freely.

The mysterious flu that had swept through affecting only the Mooonies was easy to explain away and his only regret was that so many still survived!

Now Dr Basson was so close to the final stage of his plan. A plan that had been secretly developed even before the death of Quanernia. Whilst most Quanernian's worked on the two key survival projects, one to change the trajectory of the asteroid and the other to build spaceships to relocate as many family units as possible to potential life-bearing planets. Dr Basson and his team worked on a plan to guarantee the survival of their species. This plan consisted of three elements. Firstly, to build one gigantic spaceship, called the New Dawn, which would support over 200,000 Quanernians all in hibernation. Along with supplies, seeds and essential equipment. Enough to restart life on another suitable planet, once found.

The New Dawn was set on autopilot, safely parked in orbit around the Quanernian Sun, until it received the signal that a suitable planet had been found. Secondly, it was assumed that intelligent life may be found on any potential suitable planet, one that may even threaten or destroy Quanernians, if not soon after landing, then in the months or years following. To cover this eventuality, one craft was also sent to each system containing what Dr Basson titled as the Reaper Module. The Reaper Module, once activated, the craft would be sent on a collision course with the system's Sun, causing a solar pulse. This pulse would destroy all electronic and any other advanced technological systems. Basically, returning life on any planet within range of the pulse back to the stone-age. Thirdly, with each group of crafts going to their chosen planetary system, one family had access and could remotely activate the Reaper Module Craft. There would be sufficient time for them to find a safe location.

The plan had several weaknesses, as it depended on their survival, someone had to be able to communicate to the New Dawn with a homing signal and then they also had to survive until it arrived.

On paper at least, it was the best plan they had. Dr Basson was committed to make it work!

So far, his plan was well on track. They had arrived safely on Earth. Ten crafts had landed safely and once settled they had successfully assimilated into the community. Some members had infiltrated into positions of power. Namely with Dan Mars at the White House, he was able to engineer Pat Milner, Otis and Jonsey into Altai. Also, Neil Larvarche and his two daughters Sue and Mandy were assigned to Skylab. The Reaper Module had been activated and Dr Basson's warning had been received by most Quanernians.

While right from the start the authorities on Earth were aware that aliens of some kind had landed, they didn't know how many nor where there were located. By the mid-1950's, they had become aware that a special team had been established to hunt them down and exterminate them at all costs. It was called *The Unholy Thirteen*, mistakenly based on their belief that 13 alien crafts had landed.

Up to only recently, *The Unholy Thirteen* had been ineffective. But due to the mites that they had brought with them from Quanernia, and through mutation, this had alerted authorities, not only to the deadly potential of the mites, but highlighted the need to track them down. They had then been able to track them from a combination of mite outbreaks combined with outbreaks of Tinnitus-like symptoms.

With the *UnHoly Thirteen* closing in, Dr Basson had activated the Reaper Module.

No one was more surprised than he when the Sun

went Super Nova, leading to the destruction of life on Earth. He could only conclude that there must have been some inbuilt weakness in the Sun. With such a level of destruction, he assumed that all was lost, until receiving Skylab's communication informing them that others had also been able to survive.

And now, they were nearly ready to send the homing signal to the New Dawn.

And that incompetent Dordain, could not even get that right!

He had to speak to Pat to take over this project.

chapter 47

COMPUTER LAB/
CAFETERIA (PENTHOUSE)

Even though Kaylan was initially ecstatic to be reunited with his family, he had found it increasingly difficult to relate to them. Unfortunately, his thoughts and emotions bubbled to the surface of his consciousness, and as a result they were broadcast to all Quanernians, including his family. Kaylan's mother defended him and explained that because he was young, it would take time for him to control his mind emitting. Some Quanernians thought it was amusing, but others just ridiculed him.

Since arriving on Earth2, Kaylan had completed some additional computer training and it was not long before others recognised his skill and natural flair. After a brief assignment in the kitchens, where most survivors still worked, he was quickly transferred to the Computer Lab.

Kaylan was initially given the role of sorting and filing the mass of archived information that had been transmitted to the Moon during the last hours before the solar storm. Currently this information occupied most of the available computer memory storage and much of it was now totally redundant. For example, almost 20 percent of storage was taken up with financial data along with trillions of individual transactions. His task was to determine the fate of this information. But before he could do this, he had to review and make sure that there were no gems of information or technological or medical developments that may be useful. This was a most time-consuming task. To make this easier, Kaylan developed a special search code routine that automatically scanned files, flagging those of interest for review and deleting the rest.

While not really looking for a personal relationship, especially with humans, Kaylan had found himself drawn to one person in particular. The more he tried to ignore his thoughts, the more he wanted to see her. She worked as a chef in the cafeteria, but always on night shift. Kaylan had been recently doing a lot more work on the archive project late at night and so he was also in the cafeteria late at night.

It took a long time for Kaylan to even discover that her name was Sonia, and even longer to have the courage to arrange a meeting with her. Kaylan also knew that any relationship with a non-Quanernian was forbidden and strictly enforced. He had to work so hard to ensure that his thoughts for Sonia did not emit, and so far, no one else knew.

And so, Kaylan and Sonia had to meet in secret. It took a lot of concentrated effort for Kaylan to cloak his thoughts. He was getting better at it, just as his mother said he would over time. Usually, they tried to meet in public places so that they did not arouse any suspicions and their relationship grew.

Kaylan had been consumed as to how he could broach the subject of who he was, when out of the blue Sonia asked, 'I have to know Kaylan, I can't go on like this, you know I love you, but are you one of the *Others*?'

Kaylan was taken aback at first, 'What, what are the *Others*?'

'That's our name for you. All the Moonies use it and now most of the crew of the Obama as well.'

'I've never heard anyone talk about, *Others*!'

That's because we are careful and scared of you. Sorry, I don't mean that I am scared of YOU. We fear all of you as a group.' Sarah pressed on with a concerned look on her face, 'But are you one of them? I have to know, it's killing me!'

'I'm so glad to hear that you are not scared of me, but I didn't know how to tell you, and yes, you are right, I am one of *them*. But, but, I only found out when we were trapped in the mine and I am still trying to come to terms with it myself!'

'Oh, I am so happy. At first, I thought it was me when you seemed to go into your shell. But you must tell me all about it!'

'It's a long story.' And Kaylan outlined what happened at the Bendigo mine, the Hydran Process, his family and the other Quanernians.

'Shit, does that mean that all the Quanernians know about us? You said that you are like one organism, all knowing and communicating as one,'

'Relax, no that is not quite correct, I, sorry I mean we, we can cloak our thoughts, but it takes me a lot more concentration, as I am still learning how to do it.'

'Phew, I am glad to know that! And for the first time she kissed him. 'That's another thing that you are going to have to cloak!'

chapter 48

BUNKER

Harvey was just waiting for a few to get settled before commencing the meeting, 'Well let's get started. So, Spike I think that you have some good news to share with us?'

'Indeed, I have. It is one thing to know who the *Others* are, but it is another to know where they all are at a given time. As we all know they communicate telepathically, and in doing so, we know that they transmit at a specific frequency level, given that people can be affected with Tinnitus-like symptoms. Well, I have cracked their frequency. Whilst I can't break into hear what they are actually saying, I can see exactly where they are, just like a mobile phone GPS locator.'

Spike turned his laptop around for everyone to see, and on the screen were 33 dots, moving around the base.

'Is this in real time?' asked Buck.

'It sure is, so when the time comes to take action, we will know where they all are!

'Hey Spike, one just disappeared, what does that mean? asked Nancy.

'Yes, they often go on or off, but normally only for a short period. But I have no idea why.'

'I know why.' added Harvey.

Everyone turned from focussing on the screen to face Harvey. 'Yes, they can cloak their thoughts, like going offline.'

'How on earth did you know that? asked Orley in surprise.

'Well as you know, my daughter Sonia, is fond, actually very fond of one of the *Others*, Kaylan. He has told Sonia all about them. He mentioned that he has to cloak his thoughts, so that the *Others* are not aware of what he is thinking and seeing at the time.'

'What else did she find out? asked Buck.

'Why don't we get her to tell us, she can be here in 5 minutes,' said Harvey.

With the agreement of the group, Harvey called Sonia and asked her to join them in the Bunker. She started to explain how to get into the Bunker via the access shafts, but Sonia told her she already knew!

When Sonia arrived, she told them what Kaylan had told her. Except for some obvious and more personal aspects, and then left the meeting to go back to her shift.

Once Sonia had left, Buck started the discussion, 'Well that explains a lot of things, but it doesn't really explain why Kaylan is different to rest of the *Others*.'

'It could be that growing up on Earth may explain his differences,' said Spike.

'I'm not so sure, there may be more to it than that. However, there may be a way where Kaylan may be able to provide more information that will help us.' added Harvey.

'Or could destroy our efforts if we are wrong!' said Nancy pointing her finger at Harvey showing that she was not comfortable at all with the situation.

'OK, I think your right Nancy. Let's keep a low profile on this one for now, and just let Sonia and Kaylan continue without any interference or pressure one way or another. Now, before we break up, Orley, what is the latest on that celebratory event?'

chapter 49

SECURITY CENTRE

As Security Chief, Kaylan's father Dordain, controlled and tried to manage the delicate relationship between the Quanernians and non-Quanernians. All threats were identified and if necessary controlled. His role included manipulating relationships and arranging forced marriages, all under the purpose of growing the colony. At all costs he ensured that those relationships only occurred within each group and not between them. He also knew that it was only a matter of time before the non-Quanernians discovered them and then may try and do something about it! Eventually their lack of ageing would give them away. There was only so much you could do with make-up!

So far, they had been very lucky.

But Dordain felt something was wrong, and he just couldn't place his finger on it. Over the past couple of weeks, he had become increasingly interested in the movements of the Food Production Manager, Harvey Claire and Commander Buck. They seemed to disappear at unexpected times and he had been unable to find where they went. He already had reservations about Commander Buck and his crew, as they remained a tight-knit group, which at first suited his purpose, but now was becoming a liability. He only wished that this problem had never landed on his lap. If only it had been solved as originally planned! Adding to his concerns, Dr Basson had now taken over control of setting up the communication dish on Skylab and seemed to be positioning himself to take over control of Earth2 as well! Dordain knew of Basson's reputation back on Quanernia. He was power-hungry then and leopards do not lose their spots. This Earth analogy seemed to fit him quite well, Dordain thought.

He had personally been following Buck for the past couple of hours when he went into Harvey's quarters. He used his security pass to enter her quarters, only to have 'egg' on his face when he discovered them in a rather intimate moment. He had to make an apologetic and hasty retreat!

'Gee, I got that wrong! Mumbled Dordain as he quickly exited. In a way he was glad, that they were only having an affair!

Once Dordain had left in a rush, Buck said quietly to Harvey, 'I rather think that worked well. My apologies if I did anything inappropriate.'

'Not at all Commander, shall we continue?"

chapter 50

BUNKER

Another meeting was being held in the Bunker.

'Let's start with Orley, over to you,' indicated Harvey.

'Well, there is some good news. It seems that what-ever they are doing on Skylab, it is not going to plan and it looks like being delayed even further. Dordain had been in control but has been replaced on this project by Dr Basson. Plans for the one-year celebration are now well advanced and all the *Others* will be in attendance at the time of the speeches. And that is when we will strike.'

'How can be sure that they will all be there at the same time? asked Harvey.

'I have engineered a few special awards to be presented, that's how. And Spike you can double-check at the time in case any decide not to attend and alert us. Buck.'

'The marines will secure the cafeteria as soon as we get the signal from Spike, when all of the *Others* are onsite. The Obama crew will be ready to restrain anyone from leaving or causing any trouble. We will also have four teams on standby in case we miss anyone. We will be again relying on you Spike to let us know at the time.'

Harvey then added, 'And most of the Moonies will remain in all of the core areas to ensure we control the base. I think we are as ready as we can be. Good luck and we will only reconvene now if there is an emergency or a change in plans for tomorrow night. Everyone knows what they must do. So, let's make it happen.'

The meeting broke up with everyone hoping that it would be the last time that they would need to meet in secret.

chapter 51

REBELLION DAY

Kaylan arrived to start another shift and on screen there were another 2,000 plus files that had been identified for further action by his special search and tag program overnight. Well, there's no time like the present he thought and started his repetitive process of scan and delete.

It was not until his second cup of coffee for the morning when he came across a set of unusual files which were marked 'Top Secret.' Despite multiple encryption levels, they posed no barrier to Kaylan, who broke through these with ease, and on the screen appeared a message that totally surprised Kaylan.

"This information is for the President's eyes only and concerns what is referred to as *The Unholy Thirteen*. This project refers to an alien invasion of the Earth which occurred between 1945 and 1951. The invasion consisted of up to 13 known alien crafts which either landed or crashed around the Earth."

Kaylan continued reading with interest and it mostly confirmed what he had already been informed of by the

Others, and how little the authorities seemed to know about them. He was just about to save the file when he came across the small note about what happened in Russia. It outlined that two alien crafts landed near the Vorkuta Gulag, a coalmining city approximately 1,900 kilometres from Moscow. Both crafts landed safely but were spotted by prison sentry outposts nearby. All eight occupants had been quickly captured in an old farmhouse trying to shelter from the severe arctic conditions. As with Roswell, the aliens were able to self-destruct both crafts so there was nothing salvageable. The eight aliens were transferred secretly to Lubyanka Square in Moscow for interrogation and health checks. From Gorbachev's comments, what happened next appeared to be circumstantial as all records had been destroyed, and anyone directly involved had been killed in the incident or were killed under direct instructions from Stalin. Gorbachev would only say that an incident occurred where over 200 officers died and the only way that they could contain the 'situation' was to blow up the building where the aliens were housed.

For Kaylan it explained a missing piece, that the *Others* had more powers than just telepathy. None of the *Others* had disclosed this to him. It made sense that they must have other powers which had allowed them to survive as they had on Earth. But he did not know that they also had powers to be to disable or even kill, by just mind-power. Either Kaylan was still too young or had not been shown how to access this ability. Either way he was going to find out more as soon as he could.

On double-checking the file properties, he was able to ascertain that President Pat had been the last person to access this file and had then deleted it, or so she had thought! He then saved the file in a more secure folder and continued scanning and deleting.

Dr Basson, since taking over the communications project from Dordain had been able to get it back on track. They now only needed to instal the final component on Skylab and switch it on. So, to make this day of celebration even more special he decided that he would personally take a shuttle straight after the speeches and complete the job himself. He was not even going to tell anyone until it was done and the message sent.

Dordain now expected the Moonies were going to do something, and it must revolve around the anniversary celebration in some way. On reflection, he had not been fooled by Buck's and Harvey's attempted subterfuge the other day. Since then, he had arranged for both to be followed and observed continuously ever since. To his list of conspirators, he had now added Spike from the USS Obama, Sonia, Harvey's daughter and more importantly Kaylan's 'friend,' and Nancy from the Communications Centre.

An hour before tonight's event, Dordain planned to surprise them and lock them up under the guise of stealing and profiteering. Apart from drunk and disorderly, these were the only two crimes ever committed on Altai/Earth2. So, no one would ask any questions.

Meanwhile Buck and Harvey had been personally speaking to key people all morning to affirm their support and advise them where they needed to be and what to do, as part of taking over control of Earth2. Their trigger to act was the commencement of the speeches.

When Spike advised Buck that Captain Gunn was in the Cafeteria, Buck immediately went to the Marine quarters and briefed them in full on the operation before Gunn could return. The marines were immediately on-side, as they too shared his concerns about their CO following the South Africa incident. According to them, Gunn had broken their code, God, Core, Unit!

Buck's major concern was that they had no access to any weapons, as they were officially banned on the Moon. When he mentioned this to the Marines, they all just smiled. Buck should have known, Marines being Marines never liked to be without their weapons. They informed Buck that they had disguised a crate as radiative waste and hidden a stash of weapons. While Buck hoped weapons would not be needed, from bitter experience they always helped to convince people!

Buck felt more confident that everything was now in place. He was just heading back to meet Harvey when he ran into Dordain standing in the corridor, with two of his goons. Each pointing a stun-gun at him.

'We've been looking for you,' said Dordain confidently.

'Commander Buck you are under arrest for stealing and profiteering, cuff him and take him away.' Buck knew there was no use in making a fuss as he was escorted to the Security Cells. Once in lock-up, Buck heard the procession of other 'so-called' conspirators also being locked away. Firstly Harvey, then Nancy and even more importantly Spike. The key leadership group had all been arrested. The plan was now all in tatters!

Dordain triumphantly strode into President Pat's office, ignoring the protests from her Executive Officer, 'I have arrested a group of traitors who have been planning to take over Earth2.'

'How and who have you actually arrested?' exclaimed Pat, as it was the first time she and Frank had heard of any such plan.

'Commander Buck and Spike from the Obama and two Moonies, Harvey from the cafeteria and Nancy from the Communications Centre. They were planning a take-over at the ceremony tonight.'

'Was anyone else involved'? asked Frank who had been in a meeting with Pat when Dordain burst in.

'Well yes, there are a couple more including Harvey's daughter Sonia. I have a small team rounding up a few others, but we have all of the ringleaders locked up.'

'On what charge?' asked Pat.

'Stealing and profiteering, so not to cause any undue questions.'

'Good job, well done. Let's go down and have a chat to our 'robbers' shall we!'

And the three of them left for the Security Centre together.

Dr Basson heard it all, as did all the *Others*. And instead of waiting for the speeches, he decided to leave immediately and boarded the Shuttle for Skylab. His job was far too important to be at risk now!

Kaylan heard it all as well, and he rushed to find Sonia before she too was arrested.

Just before he himself was arrested, Spike had heard about the other arrests. Luckily, he was able to give his laptop to Sonia and inform her that her mother had been arrested.

Sonia knew she had to do something before she too was arrested, but what? Kaylan would know what to do! Sonia quickly opened the laptop to see where all the *Others* were located and tried to identify which dot was Kaylan's. She saw a dot that was just leaving the computer lab and had to assume it was Kaylan. As without the laptop she would have little hope of finding him on the base. She was able to quickly catch up with Kaylan and they both hid in a nearby ventilation shaft. Just escaping in time as a couple of Dordain's security guards ran past.

Kaylan said, 'I was looking for you.'

Puffing and out of breath, Sonia replied, 'And I was looking for you. Did you know that your dad has just arrested my mother and Commander Buck and possibly other Moonies.'

'Yes, I do, but I was more concerned about you. I heard my father say that he was going to arrest you as well! He claims that you are all traitors as you are planning to take over Earth2 tonight. It can't be true, can it?'

'I don't know the details of what was planned for tonight, but yes, it is true.'

'And what were you meant to do?'

'I was asked to stay beside you and make sure we were both safe, that's all.'

'Phew, thank goodness my dad has stopped it in time.'

'Why do you say that? You must realise that things do need to change.'

'Because' continued Kaylan, 'I am afraid that you may have all been killed in the attempt.'

'What, killed, how?'

'Look, I read a report only this morning that referred

to an incident in Russia where eight of us were being detained and questioned by the KBG. It appears that we have the power to disable or even kill people, just with our minds. Don't ask me how, as I don't know yet. But over 200 soldiers were killed, supposedly relatively instantly. To stop eight of us, the Russians had to blow up a whole building. Can you imagine what would happen if there was a take-over and just one of us was able to unleash this type of power. So, you see, I am glad that it now won't happen with the leaders held in custody.'

'But Kaylan, it is still going ahead, arresting a few of us is not going to stop it!'

'Then we are just going to have to find a way.'

chapter 52

SECURITY CENTRE

Pat, Frank and Dordain sat on one side of the interview table, and Buck, Harvey and Spike on the other. Four security guards stood in the corners, armed with tasers.

Pat opened by asking, 'Just what were you trying to achieve?'

No one responded.

'You may as well tell us; it is all over now.'

Again, no one spoke.

Pat turned to Dordain, 'Take them back to their cells, they are not going to say anything now. Anyway, we all need to get upstairs for the celebration event before anyone suspects. And anyway, they will be far more cooperative tomorrow, especially when they see how we do interrogations.'

All three were taken back to their cells. They could only hope that the rebellion may still be successful.

Kaylan and Sonia had climbed through a series of ventilation shafts to the outer door of the Security Centre.

'What do we do now?' asked Sonia.

Just as Kaylan was going to respond, Pat, Frank and Dordain came through the door of security centre, flanked by a security team, heading for the cafeteria – where the celebrations were about to be held.

'Stay here until I say it's clear,' said Kaylan as he awkwardly crawled out of the ventilation shaft.

'But you don't know how many guards are still inside,' whispered Sonia.

'Leave it to me, remember I am one of them and Dordain is my father!'

Kaylan eased his way quietly along the hallway to the main door of the Security Centre. He confidently strode in whilst Sonia waited. After a couple of minutes, Kaylan popped his head out of the door and indicated for Sonia to join him. In the room, the guard lay prone on the floor and Kaylan held up the guard's security tag with a big grin on his face.

'What did you do to the guard?'

'I'll tell you later, as you will never believe it. But now we have to get your friends out of here.'

chapter 53

REBELLION

The cafeteria was almost full by the time Pat, Frank and Dordain, along with their security escort, entered the cafeteria and walked up to the temporary stage that had been construction especially for the celebrations.

Pat tapped the microphone to ensure it was working base-wide, and once she had everyone's attention, began.

'Today is meant to be a celebration of our first year together. However, there are some of you that have had other ideas. I know some of you are already guarding these doors, so that no one can leave. I also presume that all key facilities are now guarded by the crew of the USS Obama. And despite UN Regulations, they may have even smuggled some weapons.'

As if on cue, vision on the main screen showed armed marines in control in the Command Centre, 'Yes that's correct Madam President, we now have full control of the base and awaiting orders from Commander Buck.'

Pat in a calm voice trying to maintain her sense of control, continued, 'Please I would ask everyone just to remain calm for now. But first I need to tell you about us. It seems that many of you have guessed that there are people on Earth2 who are different. I think some of you refer to us as the *Others*. Before you judge us, I want to tell you a story. Our home planet, Quanernia, was not dissimilar to Earth. In fact, we are not all that dissimilar to you. Despite our best efforts, Quanernia was destroyed by a huge asteroid. To ensure our survival we sent out crafts to all parts of the solar system to potential planets. Your Earth was just one of those planets. Twenty crafts were sent, each with four crew members, consisting of a family unit. We know that seventeen arrived on Earth, but only ten landed safely in various countries. Since our arrival, we have tried to assimilate into the community as much as possible. Like many of you, we were fortunate by being in the right position at the right time to survive the solar storm. And yes, if you don't already know, we can communicate with each other telepathically. Earlier, we arrested Commander Buck and his fellow conspirators, and as such I ask you to all stand down and return to your jobs or quarters until further notice.'

'Sorry mam, I cannot do that,' replied the marine on screen.

'It's Madame President to you, and I order you to comply!'

The marine was steadfast and replied, 'I only take my orders from Commander Buck.'

'Then that is a pity.'

The marine screamed in agony and collapsed.

Whilst Dr Basson witnessed what was happening from Skylab, he inserted the final component. The satellite dish had been already set to the required coordinates and he pressed the SEND button. All Quanernians, including Pat, were immediately also aware and this momentarily distracted them with the knowledge that they were not only going to be rescued, but their future would be secure.

As a result, they did not notice Commander Buck and his fellow conspirators, Sonia and Kaylan entering the cafeteria.

Kaylan yelled, 'STOP.'

Pat turned to Kaylan, releasing her mind-grip on the poor marine, 'Dordain, get your son out of here, now!'

Dordain stood paralysed, unable to move and it took some time before all Quanernians realised that they too could not move.

'Commander, restrain all of the *Others*, and place them in the Bunker for now,' Ordered Kaylan. 'Commander?' repeated Kaylan.

'Yes, correct, restrain the *Others* and take them to the Bunker,' ordered Buck, still in shock at what he was witnessing. Between the Moonies and the Obama crew they had all been assigned to an Other to restrain and escort, as planned.

Sonia just stared at Kaylan, wondering how he had been able to freeze the *Others*.

'Once all of the Others are in the Bunker,' Continued Kaylan, 'It will make it easier for me to restrain them until we work out what needs to be done next.'

As Dordain was being taken escorted past Kaylan, he hissed at him, 'How could you betray our people. How could you betray me, your father?

Kaylan calmly replied, 'Because you are not my father.'

chapter 54

INDEPENDENCE DAY

The following day, Commander Buck was appointed the new Commander of Earth2. And further to meetings with the *Others*, a new truce was developed and they were released. The key factor that changed the relationship between the two species was Kaylan and his mother, Sarah. She confirmed with the *Others* that Kaylan's father was not one of them. They now knew without any doubt that for some unknown reason, none of the *Others* were able to conceive children on Earth or on the Moon. Their only hope for survival was to cohabitate with humans, as demonstrated by the birth of Kaylan. And now as they were fully aware that Kaylan possessed some additional and powerful mind powers. These powers were completely unexpected, even to Kaylan. He had only found out when he had entered the Security Centre and through his thoughts only, froze the guard so he could not move and was then able to induce unconsciousness. The guard had woken up an hour later and was fine, apart from a severe lingering headache.

On his return from Skylab, Dr Basson was immediately arrested, pending trial for the deaths of the 31 miners in South Africa.

Everyone now also knew that a homing signal had been sent by Dr Basson, and that in approximately 30 Earth years an alien craft carrying the Quanernain survivors would arrive which would bring a whole new set of problems. More importantly for now, they had to find a new way to survive together.

As Kaylan stared at the half-Earth just above the Moon's horizon, its rich blue colour had already started to return, he knew that Earth2 had a long way to go to survive. Its future was a lot brighter now there was the chance of healthy children between the species. Especially given that Sonia was expecting twins!

chapter 55

QUANERNIAN SOLAR SYSTEM

The space craft New Dawn was continuing its silent orbit around the Quanernian sun. The fully automated ship suddenly came to life when an incoming signal arrived from deep space. The computer was programmed to assess the signal and if it matched the criteria, it would wake the Emperor from his hibernator. This was the second such signal to be received. The first signal did not meet all the required parameters and was rejected by the computer. However, this signal did satisfy all the requirements, and so the computer commenced the lengthy procedure to wake the Emperor from his hibernated sleep. A sleep that so far had lasted just over 60 Quanernian years.

After a couple of days of recouperation, Emperor Quaylan finally made his way to the bridge to review the reason why he had been woken from his hibernation. He connected with the computer directly via his mind, communicating exactly as if conversing with his fellow Quanernians.

At first, he was disappointed, that 60 years had already

passed and that only two groups had made it safely to a planet and had been able to report back. He totally agreed with the computer's assessment of the first signal. This message was more a call of help from one group of survivors, whom it seemed would not even survive in time for them to reach them anyway. However, Dr Basson's message provided great hope and in addition by the time they would arrive the original planet, called Earth, it would most likely be habitable once again.

The computer had already set the required course and it only required Emperor Quaylan to formally approved it, which he did.

As he was being reinitialised into his hibernator, he felt the force of New Dawn's retro-rockets fire-up for their journey. As he slowly succumbed to the chemical cocktail to initiate his hibernation, he was pleased it would only take 10 more Quanernian years to make this final journey.

The New Dawn, with its 200,000 incubated survivors, commenced its journey to rendezvous with a small desolate Moon, which circled a planet which was now identified on the charts as Earth.

ACKNOWLEDGEMENTS

In the development of Nova, I have drawn upon a range of existing information and wish to acknowledge them:

1. Welsh Coal Miner's Poem – Author Unknown (From Idwal Jones of Wrexham) <u>A little miner. (welshcoalmines.co.uk)</u>

2. Colony Collapse Disorder – for more information go to: <u>Colony Collapse Disorder: A Descriptive Study (plos.org)</u>

3. Helium 3 on the Moon – for more information go to: <u>ESA - Helium-3 mining on the lunar surface</u>

4. Earth Elevator – for more information go to: <u>People Are Still Trying to Build a Space Elevator | Innovation | Smithsonian Magazine</u>

5. Earth Extinction Event (EEE) – for more information go to: <u>https://www.worldatlas.com/articles/the-timeline-of-the-mass-extinction-events-on-earth.html</u>

6. Carrington Event – for more information go to: <u>https://www.history.com/news/a-perfect-solar-superstorm-the-1859-carrington-event</u>

7. President's Emergency Operations Centre (PEOC) – for more information go to: https://www.washingtonpost.com/politics/2020/06/01/what-we-know-about-white-houses-secret-bunkers-tunnels/

8. Cerberus Protocol – from the movie 'Olympus Has Fallen, for more information go to: https://has-fallen.fandom.com/wiki/Cerberus

9. The Roswell Incident – for more information go to: https://www.theweek.co.uk/us/59331/roswell-ufo-crash-what-really-happened-67-years-ago

10. The Unholy Thirteen – for more information go to: https://www.theufochronicles.com/2014/08/mj-12-unholy-thirteen-and-roswell.html

11. President Ronald Reagan and Soviet Leader Mikhail Gorbachev discuss UFOs – for more information go to: https://www.smithsonianmag.com/smart-news/reagan-and-gorbachev-agreed-pause-cold-war-case-alien-invasion-180957402/

Printed in the United States
by Baker & Taylor Publisher Services